The Day I Began
My Studies In Philosophy
And Other Stories

Margareta Ekström

Translated By Eva Claeson

White Pine Press

Original stories copyright © 1989 Margareta Ekström

Translation copyright © 1989 Eva Claeson

ISBN 0-934834-89-X

Publication of this book was made possible, in part, by grants from the National Endowment for the Arts, the New York State Council on the Arts, and the Swedish Institute.

Design by Watershed Design

Cover artwork: duotone of a painting by Emma Alvarez Pineiro.

WHITE PINE PRESS
P.O. Box 236
Buffalo, N.Y. 14201

76 Center Street
Fredonia, N.Y. 14063

Table Of Contents

The Day I Began
My Studies In Philosophy
And Other Stories

The English Lady

Nothing turns out according to one's expectations. What good is imagination anyway, when it so often leads you completely astray? Or, was it, in the end, jealousy that played a trick on us? Well, jealousy would not celebrate any greater triumph either, at least not for any length of time.

As soon as we noticed that Chidov was happily in love for the first time in his life, we began to feel sorry for him. It would never last, we said. (Last, like sandals, or upholstery, or like the thousand-year-old pavements we still walk on and wear down every day here in Plovdiv.) Afterwards he'd be even more unhappy than before, we predicted. No woman would be able to stand him for more than two weeks, what with all those dogs (there were only three, at that particular time) and their stench, and their hair all over, and his own total lack of grooming and good manners, such as shaving, having his pants pressed, and keeping regular hours.

That's what we said, or thought in unison, we who, all of us, smelled of turpentine, had cat hairs on our corduroy jackets, and shaved only when someone from the Department of Grants for Artists (under the Ministry of Cultural Affairs) was expected to arrive from Sofia.

We were especially worried, because our dear Chidov had been marked before by the torment of love. How many of us hadn't had to stand by him that time when the fat computer operator kept him on tenterhooks for five years about getting engaged? How sick and tired we'd become of their crises, and the aftermaths of these crises, their sudden mountaintops of happiness followed by abysses of misery. We knew that landscape by heart and were not at all eager to picnic there once again.

But this was, without doubt, something different. That's what we told ourselves, experienced as we were. Something entirely different.

It started one evening in Chidov's basement. We were sitting there as usual, listening from time to time to the fantastic stereo which he'd bought (I have to stop using all these parentheses, there are too many of them but then, what is this whole story, if not a parentheses in my life, even though it's a main clause in his.) Anyway, he'd bought it cheap at our local Soviet garrison where a Second Lieutenant, not overly imbued with Marxist morality, had embellished our meager supply of available commodities with contraband goods such as transistor radios, electric razors, record players and other apparatus, and this last word described his business very well.

Anyway, we were listening either to music or to the dripping faucet in Chidov's exquisite kitchenette, where the tiles had been hand-painted by our friend Melchor, and represented either a couple of pears or a couple of testicles, the choice was yours; we called them pears when we had female company, which was seldom the case.

The faucet is a story in itself. It doesn't have a regular washer. Instead it has a couple of rubber bands. The washer was missing when the package came from Sofia, and our Plovdiv plumbers work only with larger dimensions. This was to be an exclusive kitchenette, the kind one could imagine at the house of the vice-president of the National Aviation Company. The kind of kitchenette that one showed with the same sort of pride as a genuine Gauguin, but which most often occasions greater delight, and especially, it gets the visitor to start rubbing his hands, which seldom happens in the case of good art. Also, it gives rise to expectations of ice-cubes that tinkle in a glass of vodka, or of imported peanuts that swim salty in the cupped hand and crumble oily and delicious in the mouth and make another drink necessary.

That's the kind of kitchenette it turned out to be, with a miniature refrigerator, a miniature bar, an ice-bucket and a miniature sink. The faucet drips into this sink. It makes a musical sound, and our friend Mitjkov who, in case you don't know it, was named "People's Artist" three years ago because of his completely unintelligible concert for bass violin and clavichord, has tuned his violin to suit the sound of the drops against the stainless steel sink, and then he taped (by means of the aforementioned apparatus) his duet for violin and sink. The notes of this piece are painted with beautiful winding loops on the wall where we all sit and look at ourselves sitting in front of us, so to say.

To express myself more clearly: that wall is covered with caricatures executed by the same Melchor who messed up the tiles. They are among the best he has done, and he is world famous in at least half the world. I'm there with my beret from Bretagne and a typewriter ribbon hanging down in front of my ear like a Jewish sidelock. Our friend and colleague Jordan Raditjkov sits there with his bird face and his intelligent clear eyes (he had just discovered a mountain ash tree weighted down with red berries, and instead of eating them all up by himself he is describing them so that we all become crazy about the berries and can't understand how we have been able to exist for such a long time without this northern tree). There is Ljubomir Levtje, our biggest poet, and I don't mean just in terms of weight, but also in significance, as well as the painter Radkov Chobusjka, who achieved honor and fame by his painting of the excavations in Plovdiv as they progressed, from the beginning when they resembled random bomb craters to the time of sand piles full of young archeology girls with their swelling breasts, their yard sticks and sieves, to today's excellent combinations of Roman arenas and modern coffee shops, new playgrounds and old stadiums. At this time you might at the most see five-year-old boys teasing the fat pigeons, but a few hundred years ago things were rougher: crucifixions, impalements, stabbings, living fetuses and burnings at the stake were some of the specialties. I think about this sometimes when I hear the friendly, almost caressing sound from my rubber sandals against the smooth, worn ashlar pavement, and see all around me people going about their business peacefully, unaffected by cries of terrror from the past.

That basement—it was very different from where the rest of us lived in Plovdiv. Since we were all artists, we did our utmost to live in the old town, or at least, to spend the greater part of the day and night there. The houses here are of wood, as are the balustrades; the ceilings are covered with filigree-like ornaments made of wood, and the Turkish-inspired courtyards are very suitable places in which to refresh oneself with a glass of ice-cold white wine while our wives are working in banks, schools, department stores, and insurance companies, down in the broiling hot, plebeian lower Plovdiv.

But the basement doesn't at all resemble the rest of the house, which is a typical old Plovdiv house, built and furnished by some rich merchant at the end of the 19th century. Above our heads: Turkish divans, peeling murals, ornate wooden doors, gaudy tiled stoves. Down here: modern art, modern artists, the famous wall of caricatures, and a kitchenette good enough for the Minister of Culture in Sofia, himself.

You see, it is the old and the new world. That's what we call it sometimes.

"Come on over this evening, let's meet in the New World," says our friend Chidov. For, after all, it is his basement, and the basement is situated under the house in which he works, that is, the City Hall of Old Plovdiv. Chidov is actually the mayor!

"Haha, you've never seen another mayor like me, have you? I bet you think I'm an old beatnik," I heard him say once to a couple of foreigners. They roared with laughter and hugged him. They slapped him on the back and invited him to come to Switzerland or Sweden or Finland, I don't remember which, and they became life-long friends.

That was on a day he was wearing sandals and a corduroy suit like the rest of us. Besides, he was unshaven and his gold-rimmed glasses were askew. One of the bows was held together by a lump of varnish. I was thinking they should have seen him when he recently received his medal.

Ha! What a mayor! Janus-faced, one half dark blue tailored, with brogue shoes, blue and white striped nylon socks, a close shave and reeking of cologne (his dogs growled when he came home, and he had to wash it off outside at the well in the courtyard before they would jump at him and kiss him all over the face as usual), and with a British accent as though he'd never been away from Oxford. You must agree, his other half is more pleasant. That's the half we see most of. The one that invites us down to the basement, to The New World. We sit there through the nights, and, even though the World is New, our problems are very old. They concern Art, Culture, and Women. Sometimes being faithful toward Art and Culture, and unfaithful toward women. It varies. Some of us are very young and newly married to "equal" women with university educations. You have to be very careful with them. Almost as though the women were among us.

We were sitting there one evening, the usual gang, that is, except for Raditjkov of course; he was only on the wall, not in the room, he was in Siberia or Dalecarlia, or some other such fairy tale country, looking for wild boar and hares. Suddenly, Jurij Bragdsjani, who is chief of the tourist bureau and also the head of our summer school for painters—and not a half-bad water-colorist himself—says: "Have you seen the English woman?"

Of course he said angilska dama, in our language: the English lady. "Have you seen her?"

"Why shouldn't we have seen her," Melchor with the tiles said. At this time there weren't very many foreigners around. "I think I saw her already on the first day. She came from Sofia together with two German ladies and a Hungarian. When they left, she stayed on."

"That's just it," Jurij said. "She stayed on. Before she was surrounded by her little group, like a sheep with three sheepdogs. Now she wanders about by herself, and you, well, as a matter of fact"—he almost stammered—"one just can't help—eh—seeing her."

"Is she good looking?" Radkov asked without beating about the bush. "I mean, is she beautiful?" he elucidated, so that Jurij wouldn't be tempted to go into unnecessary details. In this way he informed both Jurij and the rest of us that he wasn't interested in a description of a cute, funny, sweet or just pleasingly plump lady, here in our New World, which was a place for discussing more important matters. But, if she was Beautiful, the situation would be different. After all, we were artists and esthetes, and wasn't Beauty our main concern? That is, shouldn't it be?

Jurij didn't answer the question directly.

"She walks around here and looks lost."

"Lost? Do you mean fallen?" Melchor said, since both words are synonymous in our language.

At that Chidov opened his mouth.

"Fallen! Such patriarchal nonsense!" The room was suddenly silent.

Jurij, whose wife is a sociologist (except that in the evenings she works at home as a hairdresser, tax-free income, you know) agreed indignantly.

"My God. Fallen. That word hasn't been heard in this house since the basement was built. It's a word from The Old World."

"I was just joking," Melchor said dumbfounded at the unexpected attack. "But tell us now, is she beautiful? Or just English?"

That was when I noticed that Chidov had a peculiar expression on his face. Sort of like a cat who's been lapping at the cream, and he hastily turned around so that nobody could discover the traces on his whiskers. Actually, he just went to the mini-bar, tried to stop the dripping faucet on the way, which we all did by habit on our way to the bar, and then he took out a new bottle of this year's white wine. He made a questioning gesture with the bottle, and we all nodded in solemn approval. I examined his face. The expression had disappeared without a trace. Had I been mistaken?

The fact that he began to speak about the Bulgarian problems of distribution, compared to those of the Soviet Union, wasn't surprising. The dripping faucet often watered the flora of political platitudes. Whenever we ran out of conversation topics you could hear its calm, musical drop, drip, drip, and just as the sound of a tuning fork, it initiated a chorus of political complaining here and there intertwined with optimistic exclamation such as: "What about my portable typewriter, I got it after only seven months" or "Can you say anything bad about the combine harvesters?" The only trouble was that very few of us had ever seen such a machine from up close, or as anything more than a useful color detail in a landscape which was otherwise much too uniformly green.

Still, there was something not quite right, and I think that Melchor gave vent to the disappointment all of us felt when he, with an abruptness fit for business meetings, said: "Well, is she beautiful, or isn't she!"

"Beautiful!" Jurij Bragdsjhani said emphatically. "Definitely beautiful! Absolutely very beautif. . ."

"But not a pinup type, if that's what you are thinking." Chidov put in, and this time he forgot the washer in the faucet, which, of course, he had never used for anything other than a pretext.

Our four pairs of eyes turned to him with a mixture of amazement and regret. So, he was acquainted with her! and hadn't said a thing?

"Am I the mayor, or am I not?" He answered our silent queries. "You know perfectly well that every single foreigner comes here. I have myself given her a guided tour around the Roman arena and around the stadium, and bought her a cherry lemonade in a sidewalk cafe: I'd like to point out, furthermore, that she very much enjoyed our Bulgarian cherry lemonade."

But joking couldn't remove the serious matter at hand. He, Chidov, who never socialized with anyone but us trustworthy male friends, who didn't love anyone besides his collies, had shown an extraordinarily beautiful foreign lady around Plovdiv.

"I suppose it was when she still was surrounded by her group," I said testing.

"Both then, and later." Chidov said, and the contented cat expression returned, more distinctly now, as though he no longer bothered to hide it. That's how it all began.

When Melchor and I walked home together down the cobblestone alley, Chidov's problem came up immediately.

"You've seen her?" he wanted to know.

"Naturally, as Jurij said: you can't really avoid it."

"I can, apparently," Melchor said with a sigh. He spent a good deal of his time in a darkroom which he had borrowed from another of our friends, a photographer. There he developed photos of his newest paintings for an exhibition catalogue which was to be printed by the biggest state-owned publisher in Plovdiv. It was too delicate a job for the town's best photographer, who, Melchor said, was best at photographs for the rogues' gallery.

"She's tall and rather slender. That is rounded at the top, slender around the hips," I said. Melchor sighed again. "She could be forty, but from behind, at least, she could be taken for twenty."

"In broad daylight?"

"Yes, in broad daylight!"

"And when she turns around...?"

"When she turns around you're not disappointed."

"But when she opens her mouth?"

"Then you hear an intelligent soft voice, full of suppressed laughter."

"But does Chidov speak any English?"

"Enough."

We separated, firmly convinced that Chidov was charmed, led astray and lost, and that a foreign element, an English and disquieting element had sneaked into our close-knit Plovdiv circle.

How differently from what we all thought and feared, the whole thing turned out!

Of course, it didn't take long for the English lady to move in with Chidov. And, was she allergic to dogs? No, she loved dogs, especially collies. Did our meetings in the New World cease? No, she sent home-baked cheese crackers down with Chidov to our meetings, and he wasn't at all first to watch the clock anxiously when it got to be dawn. Was she expensive? Every month she got a check from her London bank! Did she at all intrude in his life? Only to make it better, as far as we could see.

Our friend Chidov was less and less unshaved. His corduroy jackets were supplied with practical western-type leather patches at the elbows. His hair was neatly cut, not too short—she cut it herself in the courtyard under the acacia tree—just like in Africa! His eyes shone. His dogs were all groomed. Sometimes I met her going up the steep hill to Chidov's chateau, bearing big baskets full of clean laundry, or raffia bags full of leek and asparagus. From the kitchen window which faced the alley emanated irresistible aromas of thyme, oregano and chervil, combined with and accentuated by white wine, vinegar and sour cream. We were invited to taste her borscht. Our wives ate her oven-warm scones. Quite naturally and without fuss, she took some of the best pictures we'd ever seen of the excavation and of the little students with pointed breasts who were digging there. Chidov put them into a special showcase in his study; they were admired by all his visitors, and not least by us of the inner circle.

From time to time I went to see the English lady under some pretext, when I knew that Chidov was busy at the City Hall. If he happened to come home, it didn't matter. He was so contented that he didn't even get jealous! I admired her little herb garden. It was just in its infancy, and little seeds had germinated and light green baby-round leaves had come up—I actually did get that sort of association, even though she surely was over forty. I admired, although more silently, her round brown legs on which sun-bleached little hairs glimmered, her solid arms, and the brave way in which she unshyly displayed her middle-age double chin.

No, the English lady was not vain. Nor was she cranky, stingy or quarrelsome. She was cultivated, attentive, interested. She was a real lady. And she could laugh like a young girl until she cried. (When she then roughly wiped her face with her sleeve, I noticed with the delight of a connoisseur that she didn't use mascara.)

What's more, she didn't have the slightest tendency to become hysterical. (A comment which will be worth remembering at a later stage of my story.)

Our fears diminished—and increased. I mean: there was no risk now that Chidov was deceiving himself. If there was anything that could be called love, happy love, then this was it. And, our fears increased: Good heavens, if this continued, he'd soon be married!

Was there then nothing wrong with her? What had made her settle in our sun-drenched little town and choose, from all the world's millions of men, just our melancholy mayor?

It was only much later that I understood how that very question gnawed at Chidov's heart. "Why did she choose me? What's wrong with her?" A gloomy question; a misanthropic destiny. Oh, his self-esteem was grovelling at its nadir and sullied even the loved one with the mud and mire of his self-hatred.

But before that we were to experience one of the hottest summers we'd had in a long time. The town, situated as it is way up on that rocky mountain, soaks up light and heat all day long, and becomes possibly even hotter at night when heat radiates back from the naked rock, which often is covered only by a thin layer of earth. As a matter of fact, during summer nights it is like a great big radiator, and one can hardly sit on the rock without a cushion, and no one with halfway sensitive skin would walk barefoot on the cobblestones.

And under the sun, and in the heat of the night, they loved and they loved and they loved. They looked taller, she looked more beautiful, he more dignified. One saw them in the coffee houses, never silent, always full of stories to tell and laughter. Two sibling souls, we said, who have finally found each other. On Friday afternoons, we saw them through the rear window of his little car on their way to the Black Sea. And early Monday mornings they'd come home loaded with flat fish and crabs, which we were invited to taste on Monday evenings. For they were not stingy, not insatiate about keeping their idyll to themselves. The brightest festivities during Chidov's period as a mayor took place now in July and August. The smaller ones, outside in his garden under colored lanterns, with steaming bowls of soup, in the moonlight, with wine bottles cooling in the fountain. Others, larger, more magnificent, in the courtyard of the City Hall, when the Plovdiv day sweated out all its sweet smell of wood, and torches burned around the old wrought iron well.

She stood at his side, not in his way. She took his arm because she needed to touch him, and not to pull him away from the festivities. She passed her hand over his hair, not to make him look more respectable, but because several hours had passsed since she last had caressed his poor thinning red-grey locks! We saw it. We saw and admired, sighed, and wished them luck! All of our secret fears had come to nothing. There was something pure and courageous about her. A great happiness and gratitude for him. We almost cried...

But before our first tears, or the first drops of rain—because we were all now yearning for the fall rains—there was an almost unnoticeable change. It was as imperceptible as the dew on the fallen fig, as spider threads across the opening of a mail box, as the yellow imprint one's finger leaves on the white skin of a mushroom.

Chidov didn't smile quite as much—he seemed more natural, more normal. Well, even ecstasy has to become calmer to survive. We didn't meet the English lady quite as often at the City Hall, nor doing errands. Her raffia bags were no longer full of wine bottles and onions. She didn't run like a whirlwind with the two dogs on a leash behind her. They looked very grave one day, when we saw them climb into the little car, and on Monday morning Chidov returned alone; she had gotten out in the outskirts and wandered around for hours all by herself.

What could be the matter? Had my "baby-round leaves" fantasy actually been close to reality? Were they expecting and wondering whether it was wise at her age? No, the child that was growing between them was not a child of love, it was a product of fatigue. And naturally, love did have a right to become fatigued...

It was only now that we noticed how involved we all were in Chidov's love story. We, the doubters, the sarcastic cynics, who hadn't believed that anything good could come from England, we now wished for nothing less than a happy ending. Carefully, we sneaked around Chidov as though he were hot broth and we the cats. For it seemed to us that the threat of danger came from him. From HIS side. At the beginning we started this with great objectivity, but later we cried out our disgust, contempt, and astonishment!

Couldn't he simply be grateful for this wonderful gift? Did he have a right to be so choosy? To repel and reject her? Could one possibly get tired of someone as nice, as original, as fresh, as un-demanding, as unassuming...We dug deep in the pockets of our own bitterness and came up with a thing or two with which we had reproached our wives. We held it up for examination, then shook our heads and said: No, that's not it. She's not like that! she doesn't have this fault, nor that one either. One cannot re-proach her for anything.

Was that the trouble? Was she too perfect? But you didn't need a university education to find ridiculous such expressions as "too perfect." Contradictio in adjecto, Melchor said. And we agreed.

What was wrong with Chidov? We wanted to give him a mes-sage, splash cold water in his face, rub him with scented oils, stimu-late him, cheer him up, work him up, and then return him to the path of love, shining and in top form like an Olympic athlete.

But he avoided us. He avoided the lady. He was a fugitive. Of course we still met him at the City Hall. And we still sat around in the New World. And he continued to walk through our streets with his official briefcase, wearing his rather non-official looking corduroy suit. But he was a fugitive from his inner self. The light had gone out of his eyes. He wanted to be free from happiness.

We gave up. One fine day the English lady was gone. Plovdiv, we, the mayor, everything returned to normal. The first rains came. We drove to the Black Sea to go fishing. Chidov began to look like his former self again: his face was screwed up and melancholy. The same old Chidov again. But none of us were able to say: "What did I tell you?" Because it was just this development that we had never expected.

All of this happened long ago. Two and a half years ago, that is. In the meantime I have moved to Varna, and I devote my time to the local newspaper and to the Varna district of the Bulgarian journalists' union.

Amazing how much time union activities take! Telephones keep ringing, and I stand bent-over talking into the receiver—I'm so busy and harassed I don't have time to sit down and so keep getting lumbago—and when it's not the telephone, it's the countless letters, and people always insist on gluing the flap of the envelope completely so that one can't get in a finger and must first look for the letter opener (a present from my daughter on my 50th birthday) and then not finding it, unfolding one's pocket knife with difficulty, and, without cutting oneself, start to slit open the envelopes to free the letters, which then can finally be thrown into the waste basket.

You can see that the union has pretty much kept me from being an active journalist, which has made me wonder sometimes what business I have being a member. Couldn't I just as well devote my efforts to the Varna district Union of Corn Growers, of the National Union of Rice Growers, of the Bee-keepers' Cooperative? In that case I would at least have something new to write about, and would become an active journalist once more, who most likely—as my fate would have it—would be sucked into organization life again and end up as vice-chairman of the Union of Journalists, which is exactly what I am already.

So we sit, all of us, tied to our magic merry-go-rounds, and we grow like mushrooms as dark and regular section marks on wild meadows where the grasses don't care which blade came first.

It all happened long ago, as I said, and therefore I hope that my friend the Mayor of Plovdiv will not be too angry or hurt or offended because of my writing down his story.

After all, everyone was acquainted with his earlier unhappy love life, which I have already talked about: the unfortunate long drawn-out engagement with a local girl, which managed to drag on, God knows why, until it was about as tasty as tea made out of re-used tea leaves. What you then get is only colored water, definitely not tea—and no love potion either.

The fiancee in question left Plovdiv. The English Lady left Plovdiv. I myself have left Plovdiv for Varna, but I wake again and again at night, having dreamed about the smell of wood in Plovdiv. During those warm summer nights when the town lay there having soaked up sun during God's long day—Marx's long day, I meant to say—and the heat only became more intense, because the rocky ground, the great rocky mountain which is bare in the middle of the town, like an oven, returned the heat it had absorbed during the day; on those nights the old town in Plovdiv smelled of warm wood.

It was a smell so sweet and sensual, so secure and mild, that we all felt as though we were sleeping in our mothers' arms.

It is this smell that wakes me sometimes and makes me yearn for Plovdiv, and at the same time, it seems I've never left. The smell of wood pervades the convolutions of my brain, as do the New World, the sound of the dripping faucet, and the end of the story.

Helplessly, we saw how the whole thing neared its end. The lady was as wonderful as before, as beautiful, sensitive and considerate (without any silly mothering), she was just as friendly with his dogs, just as quick, just as silent when that was right, just as successful with her herb garden, was she maybe too perfect after all? Would a little crack in the enamel have helped her, as when one keeps old household utensils, because having been used and worn out, they have received one's personal mark? Would a quarrel or a scene have rekindled Chidov's love?

But she was beyond that sort of thing. She continued to love with the frankness of a child. And Chidov, poor Chidov looked at her the way an ulcer patient looks at a table full of delicacies, the way an allergic patient looks at a meadow full of flowers, the way a love-sick being enviously observes happy, healthy love among others.

Pale and sweaty, he sat in the New World, and for once our conversation didn't deal with women; we understood without being told that that was the last of all subjects to take up.

Could he possibly be impotent? I wished that the dripping faucet would stop dripping, and that the painted tiles would only represent pears, because I was afraid that the other attribute, together with the faucet, could give our dear Chidov untoward associations.

But actually I don't think so. Had I not, with my own eyes, seen them wrapped around each other walking through our cobblestone alleys, as though they were one being with four legs, their eyes shining into each other's as though they belonged to one single constellation? And those months gone by, all those happy months before he was afflicted with this torment.

It was an impotence, a weakness of the heart, I decided. He missed his longing, his yearning. No, I'm not writing this wrong, Mr. Chief Editor, don't change anything, I'm absolutely serious: he simply missed his great yearning. He had been happy, or at least harmoniously melancholic, for he was never alone; he was always with us, his three dogs, and his yearning. That is, until She came, until Love came and robbed him of his yearning. What had become of the wound caused by the worn-out engagement, by the heart-rending divorce from the beloved? Where was the very memory of the beloved, that mediocre data operator, who was long since married to a shop manager in Sofia? She, Happiness, Love had come, and robbed him of all that and buried it under her flow of lava, and with all that fire she had burned his memory to a barren waste. And he had become a statue of ashes.

The English lady was very tactful, and considerate. To a couple of us, to me and the tourist bureau head, she hinted about differences in backgrounds and temperament, and that she, despite it all, longed for her home in England more than she had admitted. Actually, she longed for Chidov more than she could admit to anyone, but was repulsed by a climate chillier than the English, and a mystery more impenetrable than the London fog.

She had no one to turn to, and who could tell her what was wrong when Chidov himself could not?

So it all neared its end, as though this love affair had a built in biological clock, which mechanically announced: "It's over now. Time to break up."

There was no anger, no bitterness. Never even a raised voice inside the white, tile-roofed walls. The bougainvillia bloomed in profusion as before. The dogs barked happily. She handed out chervil and tarragon to our delighted wives. But finally it just couldn't go on.

I think I was the only one to witness the end. I was walking one evening after an unusually intensive drinking bout at Ramadski's, a master in leather sculpture who has long wanted to belong to our New World group but has always been on some sort of extended probation. For some reason, perhaps a foreboding, perhaps an obscure need to immediately inform Chidov of my thoughts about Ramadski (which were not especially favorable, but then that was generally the rule with this poor fellow)—anyway, I came sauntering along the dead end alley which leads to Chidov's door. On the little unfenced terrace that hangs like a swallow's nest over the precipice down to the new city, I stopped and looked at the moon while pissing in a high curve, like when I was a little boy. I had just succeeded in forming a figure eight in the air, when I heard steps behind me. Somewhat embarrassed, I stood without moving. Far off in the western part of the city I heard the crowing of dawn's first rooster.

I turned around. It was the English lady. But she hadn't come out of Chidov's door, she had come from the city below, and was going toward the door. Had she been kicked out and was she going to plead with him to be let in again? Or, had she left him, and changed her mind? All sorts of possible, more or less melodramatic, explanations tumbled around in my wine-soaked brain. But my imagination, inadequate as usual, could not possibly conjure up for me the scene that I was to witness.

A few meters from the door the lady sank down on all fours—I can still see it now despite the fact that she was in the shade of the wall, and the moonlight was hazy—the moon looked like a big poached plum. But I can see it all again any time. She looked so pitiful that I had to control my impulse to rush and help her get up on her feet again. After all, she was a lady, not a girl. Her bosom hung down ridiculously in that position, but I didn't have a chance to think so much about it because suddenly she started barking—it was high and very natural sounding, and after barking she started to howl the way love-sick bitches howl.

She stood there and barked and howled until the three dogs on the other side of the wall woke and answered her. The real and human barkings and howlings went on for a while, until Chidov also woke, got up and came out. I heard him swear angrily under his breath at the dogs who stopped immediately and most likely slunk down the cellar steps to their beloved wall to wall carpet.

But the barking and howling continued on my side of the wall and I saw Chidov open the door carefully and open his mouth to shout at the strange dog, which immediately jumped at him barking and licking and whimpering and I saw Chidov fall backwards in surprise, and I heard distinctly how he calmed her the way one calms a nervous pooch: OK, my girl, it's all right, it's all right. It's all right now. Come on, you can stop it now, girl.

After that there was no more noise, no words anymore from either human or animal throats. When I saw that the door was still open, I approached it to close it to keep the dogs from sneaking out. And I heard so many sounds coming up from the cellar (I'll refrain from describing them), happy love sounds, contented sighs, that I needed no further proof of what was going on. When I turned around to look across the courtyard, I saw that the three dogs were crowded into the dog house. I slowly and silently closed the door.

The next day she left. Chidov, pale and unshaven, took her to the taxi station. She took a cab to Sofia, and already on the next day, a flight to London. She wrote a couple of letters, Chidov told us once when drunk; then there was no more.

Crowded

No, he doesn't want to stay home and read, and get money for a movie and visit his classmate Joe and go for a walk with Mrs. Karlsson's dog. He wants to go with them.

But it'll be awfully crowded in the back seat, says his big sister, who just turned twenty. He is nine and in the fifth grade. He's youngest in the class and is saddled with the name Percy. Dad is English. That's also the reason his sister's name is Dorrit. But Mom still has her Anna-Stina, and she's from Uddevalla.

"You, he couldn't do anything about," Percy said to her one time, "you already had your name."

"Yes," Mom said, "you can't change me that easily."

Percy liked hearing that. Mothers aren't supposed to change or be changed. They're just supposed to go on being exactly the same.

His friend Joe, who lives on the same floor, has a mother who changed. The dad moved away and only comes to visit from time to time. Because of that his mother has started to drink and hang around with guys that are entirely too young. The adults call it nervous breakdown and change of life. But the boys know what it's really all about. It's love and liquor, they say, when they hear their divorced mother being loud on the telephone.

Perhaps that is why Percy doesn't want to stay home and spend the night at Joe's. Especially since they're going to visit Grandma and Grandpa in Uddevalla, even though Dorrit's boyfriend Alex is going along and Aunt May and all their gear, yes, it really will be crowded in the car. But the skis, at least, will go on the roof.

Of course, Percy's mom and dad do want him along. He is quite sure of that. It's just all that baggage: the old preserving kettle which has to be returned to Grandma, and all the ski boots and suits. It's just that it'll be so crowded. Because actually it's almost most important for him, Percy, to go along. Grandma and Grandpa say it every time they call: You must come and see us soon, Percy, we haven't seen you for ever and ever.

"There should be vision phones," Percy says, "and you could see me now, in the middle of the kitchen floor, with a caviar paste sandwich in one hand and the telephone receiver in the other and also I have blue hair."

That makes Grandma moan and groan to such an extent that he immediately has to tell her that the blue comes out in the wash. No, really, he's no punk, Grandma can rest assured. After all, he plays the violin in the local music school, and who's ever heard of a punk who plays Mozart?

Now half of him is sitting on Aunt May's lap. She had to take off her sheepskin coat and fold it and stuff it in the trunk so as to take up less room. One side of his rear end and one thigh are just about hanging in the air. Next to him are his sister's smooth black ski pants and then the boyfriend Alex. The two sit as though glued together, as though they were one person.

"And the two shall become one flesh," Dad says with his slight English accent which for the children has become the language spoken by fathers. But Mom shushes him, all reference to the fact that Dorrit really is engaged upsets her; Dorrit is too young to be either engaged or married. She has to finish her studies. She's only going steady.

"What an expression," says Dorrit. "Go steady. What do you do otherwise—stagger around?"

"Yes, or go crazy, maybe," tries Alex.

"Or, else, go down the drain," Percy says in a low voice and Aunt May says, "Just listen to him," and gives him a punch, that is, tries to, but there isn't enough room. He realizes that when he tries to get a caramel out of a pants pocket unobtrusively so he won't have to offer any to the others. He's unsuccessful.

"Sit still, dammit," his big sister hisses. Maybe she got squeezed too hard against skinny Alex and got bruised?

They have lunch at an Esso service station restaurant not far from Mariestad. Alex, who always has a lot of money—his father is in advertising, and his mother is a dentist—orders a giant cheeseburger with ketchup, onions and Boston dill pickles.

"All that?" Percy says, amazed. And then he realizes that Alex is ordering the same for Dorrit. That makes him reckless, and he orders half a chicken and a spring roll. He notices that Mom and Dad exchange looks of actually we can't afford all that, but since he's so silly and spoiled and so hungry, we'll let him.

By the time he has eaten the half chicken he is, of course, unable to manage the spring roll, and he asks the cash register lady for some aluminum foil to wrap it as a present for Grandma.

That makes both Mom and Dad feel that he is smart and thoughtful. They are glad despite it all, both of them, that they took him.

Aunt May takes out a mini chess set. The pieces stay attached by means of magnetism, no matter how much the car lurches and jolts them around. There is a strange sucking feeling when you lift a piece, a sort of tension all the way to the elbow, he feels, as he frees the pawn from that traction, and it is suspended freely in the air for a moment before landing again with a smack, for the magnetism affects the putting down, as well, hurries it. The whole procedure is a bit faster, more purposeful, somehow, than with a normal chess board made of wood, for example.

Percy gets a little carsick from looking at the black and tan pieces with the car crawling on the slippery road through the monotonous pine forest. The trees go by one after the other. It's impossible to count them. Telephone poles you can count. Dorrit and Alex have their tape player on, low. "We are the World". Then it's Leonard Cohen's "Everybody knows". He likes Leonard Cohen a lot, but he can't make out this business about living forever "when you've done a line or two". He's suspicious, thinks there is something shady about it. There is often something shady about Leonard Cohen. But that goes for Mozart as well. He remembers the movie.

All sorts of thoughts and sensations are crowding inside him now. One of the strongest is that he is about to pass out. Just before, he asks Dad to open the window on his side; Aunt May can't reach it: a bag containing a pot of daffodils and all sorts of vegetables from the refrigerator, which otherwise would have spoiled, are in the way. Snow-washed wind blows into the warmth of the car together with some frozen snowflakes. They melt on Percy's forehead. He feels their wetness and under the wetness he feels something sore. Can it possibly be the beginning of a pimple? Many of his classmates have pimples. Maybe they're catching.

Somewhere he's read that just before a war puberty comes earlier, and more children are born. He often looks at his friends' pimples and wishes they would go away. Sometimes he asks them: "Are you allergic to something?" But they only shake their heads. Some of them think he's nuts. But not too many.

When he was in the first grade there were some bigger guys who gave him a beating when he was carrying his violin case. They knew he worried about it more than he worried about himself. And he did protect it with his arms and bent his head down over it and took a number of blows and kicks. The next day he carried an old, wornout case filled with small stones and newspaper. Some of those guys got really bruised that time, and one of them lost a few more teeth than he had planned on.

Afterwards he had really been glad about the newspaper. About the fact that he hadn't made the case still heavier with only small stones. He might have been sitting in jail now. It's crowded in jail, as well, of course, but maybe he would have been given a separate cell because he was such a young murderer.

"We're going to play Monopoly at Grandma and Grandpa's," sister calls out and sounds as excited as if she had gotten two free tickets to Madonna at the Ice Stadium.

Actually, she doesn't like playing Monopoly so much, but it's become a ritual. At Grandma and Grandpa's you play Monopoly. He thinks about this from time to time: this having to be cheerful on command. Mom and Dad have their rituals as well: for example, sharing a lobster every first of March, because that's the first time they met. Or maybe it was the first time they slept together. He doesn't know exactly, he'll have to ask them sometime. Anyway, it's a ritual and they're supposed to be cheerful, no, happy when they do it. It was the first of March just recently, and they weren't so very happy. But, the lobster was put on the table and he and his sister were ordered to bed, sis took the T.V. with her, because it was obvious that Mom and Dad only wanted to sit and talk and look deep into each other's eyes and drink the sparkling white wine to each other, sis said. He only had read-out Peanuts and an age old *Scientific American*, and he thought that Mom and Dad really would have preferred to share the lobster with him and his sister. But he didn't want to say it. It would sound so—dreary. Unromantic, maybe. Still, he thought that he was right. You can sense that sort of thing in the air.

He went to Joe's for a while, and his mother was home and looked sober and nice, and they had some Ovaltine at the kitchen table and helped his mother with a crossword puzzle. That is, they had to go get different sections of the huge encyclopedia that his father had left them.

When he got home again, Mom and Dad had locked themselves into the bedroom and the lobster shells lay on the table and smelled. At first he thought he'd clean up, but then he decided that it was only by chance that he had happened to look into the dining room. He could just as well have gone directly to his room and to bed. If so, there wouldn't be any fuss about whether he had seen anything or not. Or smelled, for that matter.

The next day Mom and Dad were unusually nice to each other. And that was the end of that particular ritual.

At Grandma and Grandpa's there was always a started puzzle lying on the three-legged table in the upstairs hall. It was the table that was so easy to upset, because its three legs which were knotty branches, not at all like normal sort of smooth table legs, were held together by means of a wooden ring and then spread out again further down. He didn't know how to describe them for Joe. "Like when you play pick-up-sticks," he said finally, "and you're holding a bunch of sticks, except that there are only three. And the table top looks like an old shield, except that it is painted white."

He and Grandma sat there sometimes, and she turned on the white standard lamp that had a jointed neck like the spinal column in the skeleton in the biology closet. It was drafty around your feet, the floorboards near the balcony weren't tight. Or else it was the balcony door, the slightest little snowflake kept it from closing all the way. As long as he could remember, Grandma had talked about sewing a sort of bag out of velvet and filling it with something heavy, small shot, maybe, or sand and putting it against the door.

They weren't exactly in a hurry doing the puzzle. They held up the pieces and talked about them, and their shapes and colors. Sometimes they managed one puzzle during the whole of the Easter or Christmas vacation, whichever it was. This year, they had skipped Christmas. Grandma wrote that she had taken down a new puzzle, one that she'd bought at a museum in Gothenburg. It represented a painting by Sigrid Hjerten, more she didn't know. You had to finish it to find out what it was. It was the first time they were to do a puzzle without a model. He felt that it would be impossible—like thinking up the painting itself. Maybe you could do puzzles with the help of a computer?

Then it's time for afternoon coffee at the coffee house in Vanersborg. They always stopped there. This year the place has burned down. Surprised, they stand there in a row on the town square, shivering in the cutting wind and looking at the sooty walls that are still standing, and the chimney. They are unsteady on their feet from having sat still so long; they are warm and wrinkled. They stand there for such a long time that all the wrinkles get smoothed out by the wind, and their bodies cool off. They look absolutely pale. They stand there until Aunt May says it'll have to be the co-op then. And soon they sit at a checkered red tablecloth, they pushed together two tables without even asking, and on each table there is a small verdigris chrysanthemum and he goes around to feel them, but they are all real even though they look exactly the same. "Maybe they're cloned," he says to Alex, and can tell by Alex' eyes that he doesn't completely understand this business about clones.

"Maybe," Alex says lightly and tightens his arm around Dorrit's shoulders even more.

It's Aunt May's treat now. Sandwiches and coffee and a soft drink for him. He wants egg and anchovies, the others take ham, except for Aunt May who's different and has a cheese sandwich and tea. There's still a little cigarette smoke in the air from the lunch guests. The place is almost empty now, because they're going to close soon. Four girls with blue and white things in their hair, and white coats are hanging around in the large, brightly lit space between the dining area and the kitchen. You can see them from head to belly button, approximately. Then there's the counter with trays and silver and cash register and tea bags (black currant and lemon and breakfast) and paper napkins (you can take several to have as tissues) and saccharin tablets which are good but a little nauseating if you put too many in your mouth at the same time.

They're talking a little and resemble nurses waiting for an operation, in a way. That's how bright the lights are. At Grandma and Grandpa's they have a lot of yellow and red lampshades and candles. Dad and Mom feel that it's hard to read there, but Aunt May feels it's cozy. That's the way it is supposed to be in the country, they say, even though it is a city, the house is inside the city limits, at any rate.

After that he must have fallen asleep in the car, because suddenly he is standing there in Grandma's kitchen, and Grandma strokes his hair so gently that it tickles and then she hugs him against her big hard breasts, and it feels so good to have his head there that he falls asleep again, standing up. He wakes up because they are all laughing at him, and he has to go out to the bathroom to pee and splash some cold water on his face.

They get roast lamb, Easter lamb, and there are small yellow marzipan baby chicks in front of each plate. They forgot the daffodils in the car, so he has to run out and get them. "My little helper," says Grandma, and he can already feel it in his legs that he'll have to run up and down chasing her glasses, heart medicine, Sunday apron, the bird book, the radio and television program.

The daffodils landed in the snow outside the car, and one of them is broken. Nevertheless, they look beautiful in the window between a red begonia and a white geranium. The candles have been lit, cheeks are glowing, the marzipan is so sweet it almost makes your mouth smart. They have two bottles of red wine; he is the one who uncorks them. Grandpa takes his medicine and tells about what it was like when he and Grandma were young and were working on a luxury liner that went back and forth across the Mediterranean Sea. Everything they saw and experienced. It's new stories every time. Can all of them possibly be true?

The whole dining room has become a rocking ship. Percy had a little punch, directly out of the bottle, it was supposed to be only a sip, he's known for a long time that it's awfully good, but just then Dorrit came down the stairs. She made the bed in one of the guest rooms for herself and Alex, and Grandpa thought that Alex was going to sleep on a cot in the hall. That made Percy nervous, and he slanted the bottle a little too much.

Anyway, he is sleepy, and the T.V. movie is boring, so he lies down on the floor, under the table, which he has done as far back as he can remember. He rests his head on his arm, and his feet are preferably supposed to lie (without shoes, of course) against Mom's and Dad's feet. Both if possible. If not, at least Mom's, and she has to have her best pumps on and transparent stockings, which he used to call her summer skin.

Unpleasant voices wake him up, and he realizes that the T.V. is on. A woman and a man are quarreling. "You goddam pig," says the woman. "If you're going to be that vulgar, you might as well leave. Leave and never come back, you'd like me to drown myself, that's what you'd like, you goddam asshole. I could murder you when I think about all the stuff you've tried to make me believe, all your lies, all your excuses. How nice for you to have had a doormat like me, an obedient housekeeper to let you gallivant around with all sorts of others."

"Calm down, Anna-Stina," the man's voice says, and Percy is surprised that that awful woman on the T.V. has his mother's name. "Calm down, now, it isn't like that at all. You're exaggerating."

But the woman's voice continues just as strained and angry, "I could shred you into strips and throw you out the window; I wish the kids could find out what you've been doing."

"Not a whole lot," the man sighs.

"Certainly enough for me to hate you as long as I live," says the one whose name is Anna-Stina.

"And what about you, you're not exactly as innocent as you make out to be," the man on the T.V. says, and he sounds just like Dad, but maybe that's because the woman's name is Anna-Stina, like Mom's. "What about that guy in Orebro? And that time you were drunk at the office party?"

"But I asked you to forgive me," sobs the woman's voice, "and you said that you understood and forgave me, and it was all out in the open. That's the difference. But you, you whore around behind my back."

Percy is startled. Whoring is something streetwalkers do, only them, not men. This is something new. Then he begins to wonder about the voices and the sobs. Doesn't it all sound exactly like at Joe's house? Although the voices do sound more like Mom's and Dad's. Just when he gets up from under the table he sees his Mom throw the contents of a coffee cup in his Dad's face. She misses him, and the coffee lands on the brand new beautiful plush sofa, and he thinks that'll make Grandma unhappy, and only then does he realize what is happening.

"Shut up," he screams. "Shut up. Don't ever again say things like that," he howls. "Never in your life, or I'll let you have it!"

He screams into their white, startled faces. Mom has forgotten to close her mouth, she looks stupid. Dad's tie is loosened, and his hair stands on end. "What, you?" he whispers. All the others have gone to bed. He can imagine how they're all lying awake and listening to his Mom and Dad behind the thin walls of the old house.

"You are no longer my parents, I disown you," he says with a voice like doomsday, and he doesn't know where his words are coming from. Then he starts crying and runs upstairs to Dorrit and Alex. It is crowded but he crawls into the warm dark between them and sobs and sobs until he falls asleep. They put their arms around him. With their bodies they reassure him that they exist and that the world exists as well, even if it has cracked. Maybe it can be fixed, someday. Otherwise he'll have to manage without. Or hang it on the wall as a souvenir, as they do with cracked china.

Lilies Of The Valley

I...I...I...

Her hands grope over the bedding as though it were a keyboard. Blue-veined, swollen. Hard to make out the melody. The room is so small and so filled with her smells. Medications. Old age.

A whole room, walls lined with cheeses. When she saw them: He! He's the right man! So many big round cheeses, and her eyes as big as saucers. Provisions for the future. The flat. And everything ready. The smell of cheese, betrothal and security.

Birds fly by the window. She raises her hand with difficulty. Directs their flight in a trembling curve. Then they're gone.

The window regards her cooly and with clear eyes. Newly washed by tears. Or sun? Again and again heavy machines fall down across the sky. But when their noise sweeps through the room she doesn't know from where it comes. Startled, she calls out. But too softly. Emptiness.

She sleeps and she wakes. Whole cities pass. And villages with their wealth buried in the soil. The window shade a movie screen in the dark. Why do they keep it down? I'm awake. No, it is night.

Easy to get lost in the alleys of the night. Home: the fun place. The meadow where the accordions came out by midsummer, and finicky Kristina made her choke with laughter with her funny way of saying things. She said...choked with laughter. Rolled around in the grass, got her face full of it.

You sure are a mess girl! Reproaches shattered the Sunday harmony.

She'd just laughed. About her skirt, green from the grass. She'd twisted it around, and she had giggled and whispered. Finicky-Kristina. She could drive you crazy!

In the alleys of the night.

She'd never thought Stockholm was so big. Nor so confusing. They were both mirror and shield for each other. No nonsense allowed. The smallest of spots was examined and condemned...their judgment was hard and regulations were as unyielding as hair pulled hard and straight into a bun. Their principles were like knotty wooden floors, worn smooth and scrubbed shining clean. Scrubbed so much that their tender skin was worn away, baring the very knuckles of their clear consciences.

How the waves glittered and tooted. The boats glared with their wet sides. Their flanks. Their bellies full of fish. Capable fingers pinch and press small dimples into the pieces of fish flesh. No one can deceive her. And the mistress will be pleased.

Long nights sleeping with her head on the kitchen table. Dishes done and silver already polished. But the card players inside stay on and on. Belching smoke like a steamer. The heavy gate-key lies iron-cold on the table next to her sleeping brow. Kerchief's on and the table's as clean-scrubbed as the floor. Soon she'll hear the master's voice through the double doors. The last of the guests is to be shown down and let out. Not before she finally goes to sleep does the key stop swinging and come to rest on its hook.

Herring, smoked salmon and split open eels. Hungrily and hoarsely the boats shriek for more to fill their empty metal bellies. The shores of Lake Malaren are full of poor, starving land owners ordering barrels full of herring, wheels of cheese, butter and brandy. Do they want to eat us out of house and home?

And the alleys are teeming with little, dark men, running to fill the white bellies of the sea monsters with profusion from the stores.

It is good to own a shop like that.

How fast she walks! In spite of the cobblestones and the sun in her eyes. Walks fast? Not now. Sarcasm cuts off her recollections. Her feet are white now, like those of a princess. But she is expecting a black and imperious knight who has little interest in feet.

So fast she walks, her mind resumes obstinately. In a shower of winks and banter. Hesitating, she stops a while, fingering her purse and shopping list.

So strong they are, those chapped red hands. Her knuckles blanch and her thumbs sink into the oily mass of the cheeses as she lifts them. But her eyes twinkle and laughter flies about the market place like a sun-ray reflected by a moving mirror.

Herring brine has parched her hands. Looks as though she is wearing red working gloves. Beyond them her skin is lady-white.

"Is she sleeping?"

A wary smile passes over her lips.

The dark alleys attracted her. Madame Mansson, queen of the Old Town. Madame Fortuna in person.

There is excitement in the air long before you reach that street. She is wandering there again now, her feet cool as linen sheets.

Chilly in the alleys between the houses. As though left-over winter fog lay forgotten in the deepest recesses of July.

Where the street begins, the figure of a policeman. Face red like a sausage. Should investigate what those women are doing. But scared by the daring of his own thoughts, he makes an about-face, and piercing a sun-ray with the spike of his helmet, he disappears toward the market place.

She stands there in the chattering crowd of shady individuals. Is afraid of catching lice. Purses her lips so she looks like finicky Kristina. Nothing out and nothing in. But it is very tempting to relieve the torment of her anxiety by talking.

Her sparse eyebrows come together in an expression of anguish: "Is she in pain?"

It did hurt, in the end. Standing there, jammed on the cold porch. It had burned like blushing, deep into her soul, to yield such temptation.

Like a group of high and inaccessible cypresses, a party of society ladies towered above the crowd. If they could, they'd have their fortunes told with their gloves on. I wonder whether that wouldn't be too much even for Madame Mansson?

The window-recesses were two meters deep and a couple of women with broad behinds were always jammed in them, out of breath and complaining about painful shoes and painful lives.

Suddenly she becomes aware of the purling trickle between the clogs and high-heeled boots. The hollows of the uneven cobblestones turn quickly into small yellow lagoons. Little by little, the trickle makes its way down the steps. A miniature torrent splashes around the ferrule of a parasol. Amused, she wonders whether the woman holding its handle in her mauve silk glove suspects what is taking place between her highly distinguished kid slippers. The anarchy of pantlessness is being proclaimed there.

I didn't find out my fortune, Finicky-Kristina. What? Don't you believe in the Mansson woman? No, I don't. She lied to me. You can't tell yet, you know. You'll find out by and by.

No, she lied. I could feel it here inside.

And she beats her chest so that the whale bones rattle in her corset. An awful noise. Cars as high up as the sky. Jet planes. In the newspaper you can read about when they crash and get killed. But who is this?

"Princess Birgitta."

This is Princess Birgitta?

"It is an advertisement for stockings, Grandmother."

Read what it says!

"You will never feel as elegant as when you wear Libido's spiderweb crepe-nylon..."

Crap-nylon!

He follows your legs with glances that caress..."

Yes, he'd like that, wouldn't he! That'd suit him just fine! Skirts are to go down to the ankle bones!

They lay and peeked at us through the reeds when we were bathing. But that was innocent. Showing your ankles was worse...for goodness sakes, how short you skirt is, lass.

To think that my daughter should wear her skirt that short!
"But Grandmother, I'm Sven's daughter, you're skipping a generation!"
What are you talking about? Didn't I recognize you? I guess I thought you were Martha. You do look like her.
So many they were. Could fill the whole Old Town. Where did they all come from? And she'd pressed her lips together so hard. Nothing out. No one in. But they pushed their way through, their heads bumpy like sacks of potatoes. It hurt terribly. Took several days sometimes. But that was one's punishment for committing an ugly sin, I suppose. The original sin.
But still it's a peculiar system. To have to hurt that much! Hard to really like someone who's hurt one so much. But then, they couldn't help it, the little creatures. Did look down upon them a little anyway for being so small. Had to help them grow. Just like the man. So puny and wrinkled like a newborn. She had to help him grow. Like a child in her hands. In spite of his hurting her so.
My God, how you can dream!
Haven't done a thing for three whole days, I think.
"Three years, Grandmother dear. But don't worry about it!"
Three years! What are you saying, girl? To think that my own daughter should say a thing like that to me!
"Grandmother, I'm not Martha!"
She reaches carefully, oh, so carefully, because the body is treacherous nowadays, and a little movement turns suddenly into a violent gesture that upsets coffee cups and flower vases. A firm grasp with all five fingers relaxes unexpectedly to a helplessness that lets the water glass slide straight down onto the blanket. As though there were no hand at all, but instead a withered leaf hanging from a pain-wasted branch of arm.
But oh, so carefully now. Toward her crocheting. Which is bumpy and full of runs. Maybe it's the pattern? No, it isn't, she can see that now. The yarn is matted from her sweaty hands. Must be her

very first crocheting in primary school. Mr. Pers, the teacher, who smiled showing all his gums. And mostly when he was cross.

He smiles when he is sick of us, the children whispered. But if the slightest sound reached the red-mouthed man behind his marbled desk fortification, the long cane wandered immediately out of its hiding place to harshly point out the sinner.

He pulled the girls' hair. One of them got a bald spot that started to bleed. But her father didn't dare complain. That spot won't feed lice, at any rate, Pers said.

There he comes now to pull my hair, because I'm crocheting so poorly! Ouch! No! Please let me go. I'll crochet better right away, if you let go of my hair!

"It's the hairpins, Grandmother. The hairpins. They're all tangled up, and pull your hair."

Well, help me then, lass!

The coat seamstress lived in a flat full of frieze and moth balls. They used to meet and talk about their childhood over the hand-painted coffee cups. And Tilda's son, what's become of him? And what about Irma from Backgarde?

But on a frosty day in November, there was only a hole in the ground where the house used to be. This is where the town center is going to be, the wondering coffee guest was told. Yes, but, Mrs. Gustafsson, the coat seamstress, what became of her?

The men laughed boisterously. They didn't know that, of course.

She shook her head at such indifference, and her head just kept on shaking. There were reasons enough, really. New reasons every day.

But up the hill, there she did like going. The best view of the city. You could even see a glimpse of Lake Malaren.

She sits there now and lets the sun burn the top of her thin skull. It feels like a big egg when her black summer hat's on her knees. Inside its glass wall she sees her life. It is like an Easter egg, and all the children stand neatly in the paper-green landscape. But suddenly they start swimming around. My goldfish. Poor things. To have a mother with a glass head!

Father and mother? Where are father and mother? Have to remember to ask Martha if she happens to know. Most likely not.

The sun rolls across the sky like a round and fat cheese. There he comes now and gives it a shove. He's not too proud to help. More pale than the others, he is. No sun reaches his shop. He's white as a potato sprout, and his arms are quite thin, but strong anyway.

All her girlfriends were invited to the the potato-sprouting party. Toward evening, when the fragrances of springtime spread through the alleys and tickled your nose, he came with sandwiches and Swiss cheese. And if she smiled a little, and coaxed and flattered him, he even made the coffee. Women's work!

Of course. Of course I can make some coffee for you ladies! he said winking. It was fun, almost as though they were customers, the whole potato-sprouting party. And the oldest thirty-five.

She would then smooth down her shopkeeper's apron with her hands, and it was like a secret joke between them. She looked back at him pleased when he disappeared into the postage-stamp-sized yard to pump up water directly into the coffee pot. And he turned and winked with his shopkeeper smile, and she dared smile back at him, her lips separated just a little, since now nothing could enter through them. Here she was safe, protected by women and work.

She moves uneasily around on the bench. Has she been sitting here talking out loud? But the young man next to her goes on with his reading and turns pages at regular intervals. Won't he ever be finished learning?

Nice to sit here in this heat after all the cellar-cool of the alleys. But she feels strangely hot and cold at the same time, until someone puts an extra blanket on her. She turns her cheek to the pillow. Have been lying here for a couple of days, it seems. Tomorrow I'll surely be well again. That is, I'm not really sick. Just a little drowsy. Going to take a look at the Old Town and see if there's been a lot of change.

She does read nicely for me, the girl.

Is that Princess Birgitta?

The window shade is blue and the sun comes through in little pin-pricks. Why haven't they raised it yet? I've been awake long enough.

Carefully, slowly, she gropes for the bell. But her shoulder doesn't want to, and she sinks back. Whimpers softly like a baby chick. Will have to wait to get up then.

Was it one week ago? or two? Guess I've been sick for at least a fortnight. And so many flowers, so many flowers! So nice, people are!

"It's from your birthday, Grandmother!"

My goodness, have I had a birthday, I've forgotten all about that. I hope to God you won't get this old, lass!

"Your ninetieth birthday, Grandmother, with a birthday cake and all the telegrams that came, and we raised the flag."

Nonsense. We haven't got a flag here. Father and Mother never bought a flag pole when they couldn't afford a flag anyway. You can go ask Father.

"Grandma's father?"

Yes, who else?

But do you want me to tell you what I did yesterday?

"Well, ye...es..."

Yesterday I went up a high hill. You could see the whole town from there.

Good heavens, how small my feet have become. Am I supposed to wear such heavy stockings now, in the middle of the summer?

"Up a high hill, you said Grandmother. Careful now. Just one more step and then sit right down in the chair. There you are! Now I'll wheel you out into the sunshine."

Up a high hill, here in Stockholm...I tell you, it was wonderfully beautiful.

I...I...I...

"Yes?"

Is that a finch singing so beautifully?

"Yes."

Can you imagine, I sat there and looked down at the town and then...Her fingers fumble across the blanket, at the newspaper. Almost tear off a piece. Traitors. Miserable, deplorable traitors!

Is this Princess Birgitta?

"Yes, it is."

Where was I now? Yes. Yesterday I picked a big bunch of lilies of the valley!

Hoarfrost

Had he been wrong to bring her here?

He stretched, and the bed creaked. It had creaked during the night as well, even though the old carpenter, who died of cancer, had promised that it wouldn't.

It'll be beautiful and silent, he said and he smiled, embarrassed, like a young girl. He could still see the carpenter's face. The same man made the corner cupboard in the kitchen, and measured his father for the coffin. Same tools, same yardstick. He used to pull it out of his pocket knowingly. With it came a little sawdust, powder white. An odor of honest sweat and green wood surrounded. Soon I'll be dead, he said, matter-of-factly. That was when he made the bed. It was so wide and long that he had to make it right there, in the old bedroom where his parents had slept and which he had avoided for so long. The carpenter hadn't said anything about silence the other time, long ago, when he had taken the measurements for the coffin.

Would it have been. . . should I. . . if instead I. . . While he was thinking in the conditional the world was going on in the present. His grammar was dry as sticks and might just as well be used to start a fire. Could this apply to him as well?

His closed eyes visualized the hatches of a crematory, and he stretched again. No, he was no dry deadwood, no barren vine, no feeble little being like his dad had been at the end. His muscles contracted, he felt the warmth of his blood rushing through his body, he felt himself swelling, round like a ripe fruit, his hair thick and glossy dark brown, without a single white one.

His hand scraped across the sheet, the wrinkled linen sheet which he had found in the upstairs hall cupboard. Yellowed and threadbare in the folds. It felt pleasant and cool during the first hour, then wrinkled, soft and warm. Then he remembered: she got up early. He had tried to say "Are you dressed already?" sounding very disappointed. But he didn't know whether he really said that or whether, as though in a dream, his lips moved and other sounds came out. Perhaps he had mumbled: Put the coffee on. Or tax returns. You couldn't be held responsible for what you said in your sleep.

She knew that he was hard to wake and wouldn't be put out. She also knew he talked in his sleep, long strings of disordered words while kicking his legs and rolling his eyes. It looked awful. And how did she know? She usually lit the lamp to wake him. But first she probably lay there looking at him. Well, that was all right, he decided. They'd been together for two years now. Been together. Known each other. Made love. Gone steady they used to call in the streets when he was a child. Co-habitated. That is, she still had her apartment. Been together was probably the best way to express it. Been together for almost two years. But not every day, of course, or every night. They got together sometimes and told each other everything that had happened. Then they didn't see each other for a few hours or a few days. He had to go on business trips. She went to Varmland to her old aunt and sat there and wrote. She was a free-lance writer.

What happened when they were apart? Nothing special really. The usual. If there was anything unusual they told each other, of course. It was part of the agreement.

On the train I sat across from such a beautiful young man, she might say. Not at all as a confrontation or to test him, but altogether casually, goodnaturedly, as though she were talking about a beautiful dog or a beautiful view. He sat across from me all the way to Karlstad, she would say. At times I felt he was looking at me, and it was hard to keep from laughing.

That was all she'd say. He had been informed that she was attractive. Or else that her eyes were wide open. She saw a lot. Sometimes it was waxwings in a tree in Sture Park. And other times a young man on the way to Karlstad.

Now, today, early in the morning, as though altogether unaffected by the wine at supper last night, she had noticed the hoarfrost. She simply had to go out for a walk. Perhaps she took the car to The Ridge. You never called it anything but The Ridge, now. There was only a little bit left of the powerful boulder-ridge, and it lay there on the plain like a curved caterpillar. It was there that all that had to with sport crowded together: running tracks, trails for jogging, picnic grounds, and restrooms. They weren't the sort that made the other go along when the other didn't want to. She wasn't interested in second-hand book stores, he didn't go to concerts. They both enjoyed downhill skiing, but not to the same degree, she most. He wanted to get a dog, she didn't. He liked sex best in the morning, she in the evening, or, if they happened to wake, both, in the middle of the night. But after all, those were trifles.

His hand moved to her side of the bed again. And it returned with the same message to his heavy, warm, gradually waking body: she wasn't there.

He got up and did some half-hearted exercises, bent over and to the sides, a couple of jumps, without much energy. Obviously, this wasn't the way it was supposed to be done, his whole body knew that it was only make-believe, done hurriedly on his way to the bathroom. But still, he couldn't keep from doing it. His former wife had inculcated it into him: exercises and toothpicks. These things were so undeniably good for you that he couldn't disobey her memory, in this, at any rate.

When the water from his shower had been absorbed by the thick brown towel, he oiled his body thoroughly with unscented lotion. Only recently had he entered the warm sprays of the shower glistening, as though oiled with sleep and lust. Now the lotion had to do, a thin layer of it, a warm halo. Only recently it had come from inside, now it had to be shaken laboriously from a plastic bottle. Most likely it was after nine already, but she hadn't returned. There was no smell of coffee coming from the kitchen.

He aired and made the bed, and from time to time he leaned out the window to see the road beyond the thick-limbed ash trees. What if she had slipped and broken a leg?

He took his cafe-au-lait at the kitchen table and lit the candles— four new candles, now after Christmas. They were red. She would certainly be here any minute now, so he set the table with the blue and white breakfast cups, took out lots of bread, both dark sour-dough and white for toast. A mild cheese on the china platter. Cottage cheese straight out of the package, even though that was an affront to his sense of aesthetic. Rusks in a basket, actually the bottom part of a Chinese bamboo basket used for steaming dumplings. Nature-pure honey, orange marmalade.

He sipped his coffee and finished setting the table. The chairs felt winter-cold, the house stood directly on the ground, and the cold rose through the chair legs as though through capillaries, radiating to the seats. He went to get two sheepskins from the sloping, narrow cubbyhole under the stairs, where hunting rifle, empty jam jars and folded canvas chairs crammed together with a moth-proof bag containing his student tuxedo as well as his mother's old wedding dress. He had written FREUD in big black letters on the bag the time he had come home after graduation from the poly-technical school, engaged to a psychiatrist. He had wanted to please her by doing a little analysis on his own.

Now the sheepskin lay there waiting, on her cold chair. The slices of bread were starting to dry; he took out a clean kitchen towel and covered them. Then he went out to the courtyard.

At the neighbor's, a surveyor, the dog started to bark. He used to go along on hunting trips. He walked away rapidly so as not to raise unnecessary expectations.

The mountain ash stood straggly and black against the white fields; every single berry lay in the stomachs of magpies and thrushes. But the dog-rose bush was full of enticing lipstick-red fruit, each with a snow-white cap. He would have to show her this. If only she would come back. He looked searchingly across the wide fields. A yellow streak of reeds showed where the creek ran. Toward the horizon in the west, the spruce forest stood dark. That's where the ridge began.

The sky was as colorless as the snow; only a road sign shone like a sunflower. No one was out walking. The farmer's sheep climbed up on a snowbank and chewed and stared at him.

Snow had fallen during the night. He saw tracks from a cat and from the surveyor's family with their dog. Where the dog had piddled the snow yellow and porous, the tracks turned back. But something else went on. Suddenly he realized that he was following her tracks. He had tracked her down. The narrow-toed boots that hurt her but that she persisted in wearing. He had wanted to throw them out, and then buy her a pair of sensible ones lined with sheepskin instead. It was their tracks. She had taken long strides. Had she been in a hurry to get away from him?

He stood still and considered whether he should shout. But just here the road followed the creek more closely and you could hear the water gurgling under the ice. His voice would not carry far.

He looked around. The fields. The sunken fences. The avenue of whitebeam trees leading nowhere since the dark red homestead that belonged to the chaplain burned down, last year. The two farmyards further on, referred to as the village, even though they were only two and belonged to brothers. Toward the horizon, for the road had turned, lay the factory with its silo and brickworks, manorhouse, chapel and rows of red workingmen's cottages. Beyond, there were some clusters of two-story cottages around the co-op and the public baths.

On the main road the cars began to come alive little by little as the sun rose behind its misty window. But no one was walking with either long strides or short steps. There was no living being in sight. Only the tracks went on.

He thought about the coffee—had he turned it off? And what if she had walked the round as far as the turning point and was returning behind him and then wondered where on earth he was? Hoarfrost lay thick on the telegraph and electrical wires. The birches looked like handmade lace. The snow crunched under his shoes. He wondered whether it crunched under her boots as well.

But she had not turned off in the direction of the main road. Instead, she followed an unplowed road that went through a small copse of hardwood trees and lead to the deer hunter's cottage. A deer hunter lived there in the middle of the nineteenth century with his deerie and his deer kids. That's what the boys from the brickworks used to say when he was little, trying to be funny. Then the place had been turned into a summer cottage. Now there was a T.V. personage living there, a celebrity, the sort you see on the screen just about every week, almost a culture personality. His specialty was dialects, he traveled around and taped people. But he turned up in many other connections, as well: environment, the evils of spanking children, independent theatre groups, fluoridation of water, housewife pensions and "give us back our greetings telegrams." No discussion was beyond him: he had the gift of gab.

He was a nice enough guy, said the surveyor, who had talked with him while standing in line at the bank and at the co-op. Others understood his wife had left him. Here in the country he kept a low profile, one could say: he drove a Volvo, came to the bonfire on Walpurgis night, carried home state liquorshop bags from the tobacco shop and behaved like everyone else. The only thing that was different about him was that he lectured at the housewives' club last Christmas, and the parson asked him to make a speech at the midsummer festivities.

This is where she had turned off. In the direction of the deer hunter's cottage. But she wasn't really the inquisitive sort. True, she had mentioned that he and she had taken the same course once, History of Art, she thought it was. But she'd never seemed to want to meet him when she found out that they were neighbors. On the contrary.

He had a tingling feeling in his stomach, like when a dressmaker impatiently pulls two drawing strings together. What he should do now is turn around and go home. Watch television. Take a sauna.

Prepare lunch. There was a whole lot he could do. She'd come sooner or later, after all. She wasn't a reckless sort of person.

Just before the road came out of the copse he stopped. It made a small circle. Perhaps the loggers had piled their logs there. There were tracks of a caterpillar tractor, cars and horses, covered with new snow. The text was confusing, partially erased. He wasn't about to take out any magnifying glass. He was going home to switch on his sauna. Or the television. He couldn't make up his mind this far from the switches.

Here, at the edge of the woods, you could see the deer hunter's cottage. Its smoke, thin and fuzzy like a pipecleaner, rose perpendicularly into the grey. The celebrity was home.

He turned on his heel obstentatiously making a little round hole in the snow. That was when his left eye caught sight, almost indirectly, of something blue on the path. It stuck up out of the snow. A glossy piece of cellophane with print on it.

He started and a series of memories went through his head while he swung round on his heel again. It was the most popular brand, all right. But it was certainly too damn cold for that outside, on a day like today. There was hoarfrost, after all!

The scrap of paper lay there and stared at him. The bit that stuck out the snow was hardly bigger than the ear of a mouse. It would take him two seconds to pick it up and verify that it was what he thought it was. But what would that prove? Anyone could walk, stand or lie here, against the trunk of a tree, or in a car, for that matter. And it was perfectly possible to drive in and turn around here with a car, he had just realized.

He stood as though frozen to the spot, the film was stuck. Then two sensations hit him: a sort of gentle joy and bitter pain. At the same time. As though being slapped on both cheeks simultaneously.

The strange joy was stronger, he was almost exhilarated as he made for home at a half run. His black boots thundered against the snow, which rose feathery-light from the ground like Hermes' wings. Was he the spirit of retribution or the apostle of lightheartedness? He could be furious and leave her. He could also be free to do likewise. And besides, perhaps it wasn't she. Of course it wasn't she. It wasn't like her. And was it like the other guy, the celebrity—how could he know? And who was like what or whom? Where did the likeness stop? He knew nothing about that either.

Full of uncertainties, he stamped off the snow on the porch, and shouted a resounding "Hello, darling!"

But that was a mistake. You couldn't be furious after that sort of play opening. But suspicious. Wiley. Calculating. Should he say he had been somewhere entirely different? Yes, of course. But didn't that already mean that he was playing their game?

No one answered. The kitchen towel lay where he had left it. A newly-hatched winter fly thudded against the window; he let it out, it took a few deep breaths and dropped like an inkblot on a white sheet of paper.

He warmed the coffee and went to get the newspaper. He had almost forgotten his walk, engrossed as he was in an article discussing faulty insulation of wooden buildings—the subject matter of his Ph.D. dissertation had been the insulation capacity of wooden walls under extremely variable conditions of temperature—when she suddenly stood there in the middle of the kitchen floor. Her eyes sparkled deep blue, a few snow flakes were melting in her bangs, her cheeks were glowing: "Oh, I'd love some coffee!" she said with her soft, almost purring voice, and her big smile right away made him smile as well.

"Where did you go—apparently very far!" he said, and now his stomach muscles cramped strangely again.

"Yes, but not too far," she said, and sparkled a little extra so as to cover up the stale old joke.

"Would you like some toast?" he said and was amazed to notice that his hand holding the slice of bread was trembling.

She was bending over in the hall pulling off her narrow-toed boots. "Yes, please," she said in a strange voice, because of the exertion. "Two slices, please. I'm so very hungry."

He felt hungry too when he looked at her bent over like that. Is she really hungry, he was thinking, or instead very satisfied. Or, had her appetite simply been stimulated?

"Was it nice?" he wondered and pointed to the chair which he had covered with the sheepskin for her. But she sat down across from him, as she usually did in his apartment in town, with her feet wedged between his without being aware of it.

"Ye-es," she said with conviction. "It really was. But I almost lost my way. When I got to the main road I was sure I was supposed to keep to the right. Didn't you say, yesterday, that you could make a circle and come back here? Well, that's wrong."

He put his sock-clad foot on her lap. Something worried came into her eyes, and he recognized the look. Her eyes were fishing for something in his own, like the hand of a child searching for candy in a caramel-sticky pocket.

They were very silent.

"Shall we have our coffee afterwards?" he wondered and felt how she moved her legs a little so that his foot sank down comfortably between her thighs, his heel resting on the seat of the chair.

"Yes," she said in a low voice, quickly wiped some crumbs from her mouth and rose, obedient like an office girl when her coffee break is over. And then she said "Yes," one more time when his grey sock-clad foot thudded to the floor, and he stretched out his arms to reach for her.

* * *

The T.V. holiday movie wasn't quite as funny as advertised. Movies from the thirties seldom were, whether this had to do with their pace or the fact that they were black and white. They sat there yawning on the low, flowery sofa in the living room. Where the T.V. was now, his parents had the old radio in dark oak veneer with an illuminated map of Europe, on which the radio station you listened to glowed like the red head of a pin. It was never other than Stockholm, Berlin and London, as far as he could remember.

"Don't we have any," she started, but changed to: "Isn't there any candy in the house?' '"

"No-o," he said and kissed her ear lobe, "we don't have any candy in the house." That was the closest he would ever get to a proposal, and they both knew it.

"I'll go and see," she said, raising herself a bit clumsily from the sofa, "if I have anything in my coat pocket."

She disappeared in the dark hallway. It was snowing again. The candles in the window lit up a little of the outside where snowflakes appeared and disappeared, appeared and disappeared in an irregular, diagonal rhythm.

"Look at what I found!" she shouted, her voice sounding like a school girl's, and holding up a plastic bag with caramels. He quickly put together her clumsiness and her overly cheery voice and thought: I hope to God she won't sound more childish the older she gets; this is definitely about all I can take.

She sank down next to him and they peeled the dark blue cellophane with print on it of the caramels and inserted them between their lips, which were still sore from that morning's love making.

Thoughtfully, he folded the blue cellophane to one centimeter in size, and then smaller and smaller until it was a small tube, blue and shiny like the body of a dragonfly.

"They really taste good," he said. "When did you buy them?"

"This morning; didn't I tell you that I walked all the way to the factory, to the kiosk?"

"No-o, that you didn't tell me. Only that you'd been far."

She could just as well have gotten them from the celebrity, he was thinking bad-temperedly. And why should it just be this sort of paper I saw in the snow? And how had she gotten there if she'd first gone to the factory? And in that case, who had given her a ride, and who used condoms and who ate caramels and...it was an impossible road to follow.

"What do you do when we aren't together?" was what his mouth managed to say.

"What do you mean? Do? There's lots. What do you mean?"

"I mean: what do you think about?"

"About you," she said in a low voice. "I think a lot about you."

"But not all the time?" he continued.

"No-o, not all the time," she said and laughed.

And he felt that if he asked one more question, it would be more and more seldom.

The Day I Began
My Studies in Philosophy

What is a housewife supposed to do when her children are almost grown, her periods have ceased, and a new woman has come into the picture? Go and hang herself in the attic is an excellent suggestion, but the ceiling in our attic is so low that I would have to hang myself by the knees. Registering in art history at Stockholm University is another good suggestion, but terribly unoriginal and stale, which is exactly what I feel I am.

"You have to be more philosophical about it all," my husband said when I rolled around the kitchen floor, pulled out large tufts of my increasingly grey hair, and kicked a hole into one of the exclusively elegant Poggenpohl drawers. "You have to be more philosophical about it—some people simply get run over, it's not the car's fault!" (He used metaphors from his line of business.)

That's when I decided to begin my studies in philosophy.

It was a day in early August, the month when the old school year begins ticking in all of us who didn't get enough, and when peoples' souls, like migratory birds, yearn for new itineraries, preferably in a flock. Actually, I've philosophized ever since I was a little girl: about creases in my top sheet, and whether it would be possible to call forth very small skiers on the Persil-white slopes; about the yellow stains in papa's bed, and where they came from; about the scars and ridges on my still young knees which came so close to my eyes when I was perched on top of the woodpile at Grandma's house and heard her singing; and about why I was slapped when I said I wished I could have a pair of green shoes.

Little by little I had managed to philosophize about the very meaning of life, as well as the meaning of the fact that there also were boys; about the nature of flowers and the deceitfulness of water-colors; about the fact that eyes could see more than hands are able to draw; about the roundness of apples and the protuberances of the sun; about the tendency of small children to grow up very rapidly and not in the least, and this, for almost two decades now about my unbelievable luck when I found THE MAN in the crowd at St. Erik's Trade Fair, where I was demonstrating typewriters for the Japanese company which I now head, and where THE MAN came, arm in arm with his young wife, to see new models of kitchen stoves.

Then everything changed very rapidly, but not at all painlessly, into new models, and they were him and me, him and me, year in and year out. At least I thought so, until a month ago. That's when I understood that there were more people in the boat and that it was about to capsize.

"Sit down in the boat!" Grandfather used to roar when we fished for crawfish in Lake Vin. And I would sit still until I felt my rear end grow fast with the grain of the thwart and my feet become firmly riveted to the seaweed-filled bottom of the skiff. You can make yourself heavy and solid, and you can make yourself light and flighty. For me to evaporate now, like fog over a meadow, is my husband's dream (or perhaps he sees me more like exhaust fumes). But I make myself heavy and sticky. I mess up things and snivel and whine. I am a snail, the size of an elephant, which he looks at helplessly. A little philosophy would do no harm.

At work I didn't say anything about my plans, nor did I at home. When I took a course in Spanish a few years ago, people around me seemed to consider it as part of my menopause. Afraid of being asked: "What's the point of studying philosophy?" I sat silently at my desk and dialed, time and again, the telephone number of the University. They were busy there, of course, at this time. I could visualize the students standing in line, but for the sake of my employees' morale, I never left the office during work hours. And so, I continued sitting at my desk, dialing over and over again. Suddenly, one morning, I was connected! I could feel my legs trembling and my cheeks blushing. The switchboard operator managed to repeat her "University" two of three times, and the third time she sounded quite angry. I finally got out: Philosophy. . .I thought I'd like to study philosophy. "You can talk with the student advisor between 8:30 and 9:30 a.m. tomorrow. It's too late today," she said. And there wasn't anything else for me to do than to hang up and accept the fact that this wasn't the day I would begin my studies in philosophy.

The next morning I left home at the usual time. By eight thirty I am usually at the office, most often I am the one to open the door. Leonard from the warehouse comes a little later and rattles the noisy sheet-metal door in the courtyard. He usually whistles so loudly that you can hear it all the way to the office on the second floor of our little 19th century building on Jungfrugatan. Between the warehouse and the office there is an importer of hides who is rarely there. He's probably out hunting.

This morning I turned off the freeway and headed for the university instead. The long, ice-blue blocks of building lay in the midst of a little woods and didn't fit in. I had seen them before, even from the inside, because a cousin of mine had worked there in the seventies teaching Swedish to foreign students. But this time I came in an entirely different capacity. As an adult student. I could feel all the delicious exhilaration that I had felt such a long time ago when I registered at the old Stockholm University, afraid of everything and everyone but also curious and thirsting for knowledge. It turned out to be mostly economics and boys that time, then I landed at the firm, got married and had children. Now was very different. Now I stood on the threshold of loneliness or of a new life, and as far as men were concerned, I knew too much. Philosophy, on the other hand, was something I knew too little about.

There is a large parking lot below the university, and there were lots of spaces. I left my blue car unlocked, because no one else would want it. I had the morning paper under my arm, together with a folder dealing with the new personal computers and electric type-writers we will be selling in the spring. Small, thorny bushes lined the steps; they looked as cloned and rationally designed as the tall university buildings.

From close up the buildings seemed less rational: an extremely insecure construction of plastic or glass tiles that were held in place by ugly and possibly unreliable screws. The steel girders that sup-ported the canopies over the entrances were so rusty that they seemed porous. I managed to open a door and found myself in a long, very narrow corridor with about ten closed doors on each side. Was I in building D or building E? Suddenly I couldn't remem-ber; after all I had so many other things to think about. "You've got to be strong! I wish you were strong!" the man in my life shouted when I stood sobbing on the steps, folder and car keys in my hand.

"Strong enough to stay or go?" I sobbed. This, he thought, I could easily figure out by myself. Was it a rhetorical question? Ac-tually, I am strong, I thought at the time, but wisely enough, I didn't say anything. I am strong in my yearning for you. And my love is strong, as well. My love for you.

But I didn't say it, which doesn't mean that I hadn't uttered much worse sentimentalities on other occasions, enveloped him in a Nessus tunic of unrequited love and then pulled and tore so that bits of flesh and skin came off, and he left the house screaming in horror.

This time I just wiped my tears with the back of my hand, a movement that has become as familiar as quickly raising myself to my toes to give him a kiss had been a couple of weeks ago, and before those weeks, for almost twenty years.

I just wiped my tears and, with forced good humor, said: "See you later!" In what they call The Great Love, there are those who are black and those who are white. The whites are the rulers and the masters. Between them and those who have become soiled and blackened with love, there exists a state of apartheid. It takes a while to remember all the rules, and you practically never have your passport with you. Not that it makes any difference: it expired a month ago.

As a matter of fact, I met a couple of black, or at least brown, people here at the university, in the long, narrow corridor. They wore dark red t-shirts and very tight jeans and seemed to be part of the cleaning staff. If that was the case, they obviously were off duty, since cigarette butts and candy wrappers were dancing around at my feet. There was a door open to one of the two rooms: two East Europeans sat on a table speaking their incomprehensible language with a Swedish teacher and an interpreter. The conversation sounded heated. A young man in a sleeveless T-shirt, sort of like an undershirt with large sweaty stains under the arms, had been ordered out by the woman, and was wandering around in the corridor. I wondered which department they were in. Then I reached the next corridor.

Contrary to the one I had just walked through, this corridor lead from one building to another, a connection. Also, here all was relatively dark and littered. Some of the red Masonite tiles on the walls were loosening and the smell emanating from a door titled Men's Room wasn't exactly one of sweet violets.

I was definitely lost now and pressed my morning newspaper and the folder with the new models harder under my arm. If only there were a new model for our love, I mumbled to myself. For, for several weeks now I've been talking audibly to myself, and here in this corridor there was no one to hear me anyway. Like with atoms and molecules, new compounds. But I sure don't the hell know whether I could stand having her around so damn close, I grunted to myself and wandered on. I didn't know whether the unsupportable tension I felt in my lower arms was caused by the beginning of school, jealousy or the morning paper and the folder. Anyway, I walked faster. But I forgot to breathe for long periods of time.

And even if he should make some sort of arrangement, if he should try to communicate again, bring us nearer to each other, nearer my God to Thee, . . . I continued, within me, all is still unresolved. And so I wandered and mumbled on.

It said Smoking Room and Café on a door. But not Student

Advisor, or Philosophy. I realized now that the sign about smoking or not smoking had been quite frequent in the first corridor. There had even been a diagram for the existing smoking areas in all of the buildings, sort of like those in airplanes or hotel rooms for emergency exits and fire escapes.

This is where you're supposed to smoke I thought, and decided immediately to make it opium. It makes one forget and works most philosophically. I could visualize myself sitting crosslegged on a blue silk cushion, smoking while being taught philosophy by a handsome young man in a soiled undershirt who didn't use all of his energy to keep me at a distance.

Sometimes I mimic her, and I have to watch out, when walking in long empty corridors, that I don't unconsciously slip into the role. You see, I make fun of her, of the way she talks, laughs and looks. When he sees me doing it, my husband looks at me sternly and kindly at the same time (he has ancestors in the clergy, and is actually the first car salesman in the family) and says: I know her. I know perfectly well what she looks like.

That gets me confused, embarassed and apologetic,like a person would who's laughed so hard that she's dropped her false teeth. Clumsily I put them back in place and resume my habitual, worn out appearance and slink off. I've done my bit then, whatever it is good for.

At this point, I was slinking along the corridor, through smoking rooms and cafés, by green and red tiles that were about to loosen and fall down on top of me, by interminable bulletin boards for law school and social sciences where young girls with tight curls stood and scratched their heads with their pencils while watching young men also, in vain, looked for important messages under the headings of law school and social sciences. In a couple of meters of empty space there was a handwritten poster, on which it said Staples. Professor Staples was obviously extremely busy, this term, I decided.

Since, by now I was so lost that it made no difference whether I was there at all, I could just as well return to my first method of approach to the university and the subject of philosophy: that is, to phone the switchboard.

I found my way up to the ground floor, succeeded in opening a locked door, and was outside in the open air. I realized that the door was not supposed to have opened for it fell shut and locked behind me, but I quickly walked away and tried to look as though I had come from somewhere else.

The relief of getting outside could only be measured against my enormous longing to get inside, most of all into a philosophy class. Already after about ten meters an opportunity presented itself and once more I crowded into the somewhat dilapidated student factory. Of my own free will. Nevertheless, the thought did go through my head: my car is down there, and the gas tank is almost full.

If I whiz off I can be at the office within fifteen minutes. Or why not in town or in the Old Town? Or on the freeway going south, like that poor lady in one of Klaus Rifbjerg's novels, the one who keeps on traveling until her middle class make-up wears off, and she is surprised to see the freeway end in Portugal.

I am pretty strong as far as fleeing is concerned, Buddy! I say this brazenly, addressing myself to my husband. But I had actually never ventured outside the magnetic circle of our residential neighborhood, and, up to now, I've been like a little boy who's about to run away from home, and reassures his mother: "But I'll be home for dinner!" And usually, in those cases, my husband bought a treat for dinner, to console himself or me, who knows which. Perhaps it didn't make any difference.

Something always pulled me back to the ugly yellow-brown house. A strong force. Or was it masochism? But if I whizzed off now, I'd make it, I think.

Unfortunately I now arrived at a populated part of the university and was forced to rearrange my face: no more mimicking, no mumbling to myself, or shaking my fist. I was passing a well-lit kiosk and some candy hungry future students who had turned around with great astonishment when they heard me shout Buddy! in a pretty loud voice. They didn't, after all, know what my situation was.

There was also a whole series of arrows saying "Telephone" and "Toilet" and also, and that was what was new and surprising, one arrow announced "Student Advisor." Delighted, I followed the direction in which the arrow was pointing. With my heart beating wildly, I went down a flight of stairs and entered a corridor. It was a long corridor that went by a door labeled "Caretaker." As head of my office I don't have entirely pleasurable feelings about the concept: caretaker; it immediately brings to mind the increase in rent for our storage room even though the caretaker had never bothered doing anything about the leak and thought we were joking when we told him that we had to put out plastic buckets every time it rained.

I did have a hard time keeping my thoughts together. Philosophical discipline was what I needed. But I had reached the end of the corridor after having passed new and empty bulletin boards and again others with Law School and Social Sciences, obviously very popular subjects. And now I had arrived! Clear as crystal, it said "Student Advisor." Actually I didn't really want so much advising, what I wanted was simply to register so that I could begin my studies in philosophy. But how on earth was one supposed to go about that?

Through an open door I saw a busy lady dealing with a difficult case. "Yea, but what'm I sposed to do if I haven't got a stipend an' no papers to. . ." "In that case you have to get your papers from your home address," the lady said with careful enunciation. "But, don't you see, I've moved," the girl continued with her difficulties, "an' it isn't dead sure that they've got my papers yet, and what'll I. . ." Her sentence hung there like a stretched piece of chewing gum and since I wasn't looking for financial help, I turned decisively toward the other door, the closed one and saw that under Student Advisor there was a smaller notice in red: Only between 1 p.m. and 4 p.m. Please observe our office hours!

I walked away and wondered somewhat about what the lady on the switchboard had meant, and why no one observed my hours, and that it was apparently like getting into heaven: the thing to do was to force your way in. It was obviously something you had to feel stoical about when you were practically a philosopher.

So I walked back the same way, because near the kiosk I had seen three public telephones. The best thing would still be to phone the switchboard lady right here on the spot even though she most likely sat somewhere very close, perhaps behind one of the many closed doors I had walked by. (Still better, of course, would be if she simply could provide the instruction, but that would be too much to hope for.)

The first telephone, complete with its perforated Masonite booth, was out of order. It had been reported, it said, so that I wouldn't be tempted to do something about it by way of the remaining two telephones. One of them swallowed three of my remaining four one-crown coins without giving me back any of my money's worth. While I was working on the third telephone, dialing the old familiar switchboard number, a young girl arrived at one of the out of order ones. She seemed rather nervous—should certainly take up philosophy, I thought—and started to manipulate a telephone catalogue. She uttered something guttural that I understood to mean: Oh, maybe you need this, how stupid of me... So I said truthfully: No, of course not, it's all yours. To which she answered a pretty angry What? But by then I had already reached the switchboard and while studying the various engraved pricks with and without text, the telephone numbers and the misspelled obscenities, I said to the woman's voice on the switchboard: "I would like to begin my studies in philosophy. Could I please speak with a student advisor?

First she didn't understand what I said and I realized that I was tired and probably had spoken unclearly. At this point the girl next to me discovered that her telephone didn't work and that made her communicative. "This telephone doesn't work!" she told me, as though I didn't already know it. Besides I already had another one that worked. "Wait a while and you can have this one," I said kindly and it occurred to me that I really seemed quite old and motherly in this place.

The switchboard operator thought that I was speaking with her and yelled a furious, "Whaddayou mean?" And I had to repeat the whole thing about philosophy and student advisors. Where can I find a guru in this dreary dale? And then she connected me and while the girl who had said "What?" left looking absolutely happy, as though she had managed both to make her call and find out something funny, I stood there and listened to the distant small seals that howl and howl in the furthest reaches of space. After a very long while the operator came back and said: "There's no answer." "When can I reach them?" I wondered. "Who? Who do you want to talk to?" she said, and I decided that they had changed shifts while I had stood here and looked at pricks with and without wings and female organs that were smooth and enigmatic as almonds.

"The student advisor," I said. "The Department of Philosophy."

"Oh dear, I connected you to the wrong extension," the operator said and tried again. But before she managed to call forth the small seals she returned to my listening ear and said: "The student advisors in the Department of Philosophy will be here tomorrow at 1 p.m."

When I got outside I saw my little blue car standing in the distance. I hadn't been so happy since that time long ago when I unexpectedly met my six-year-old son walking on the street looking into store windows like just anyone else, because he had a free period, and I stood completely still, next to a tree, just looking at him until I, of course, couldn't stand it any longer and ran out and kissed him, to his embarrassed delight.

I didn't kiss the car. I stood next to it and took a very deep breath. I wondered a little whether it would really be possible to study philosophy surrounded by all those cigarette butts, hand-painted pricks, steel-tube furniture and off-duty cleaning staff. But then again, you could always go to the kiosk and buy candy. Or sit in the bodega and drink French country wine. After all I wasn't planning to burden the budget of the state with any subsidies toward my education. I was only a very sad female business manager who wanted to manage something for herself.

That evening my husband and I were invited to a party. I showered and changed and although I knew I shouldn't say it, knew it so well that it was almost as though I hadn't said it, but finally I yelled: "What about her, isn't she coming too?!"

He looked at me with a hurt expression on his face. He's become sensitive from all the flogging. I can understand that. That is, sometimes I think that I should be able to understand it.

That question and the hurt expression on his face, an expression of, so to say, hurt guilt, didn't, for once, start me off rolling on the floor, tearing out my hair, kicking over innocent piles of newspapers, throwing away completely fresh and healthy flowers, screaming so loud that all the time it was going on you hoped that the radio was giving something similar for the sake of the neighbors.

No, we just stood there and looked at each other for a while, and I put my arms around him and held him tenderly against me. I felt him resisting slightly, a negative charge, and it made me think of those small Scottish terriers, one white and one black that I had when I was a child. When they sniffed each other's snouts they were united in a magic kiss. When one of them sniffed the other in the behind they flew apart. I remember the mysterious feeling in the tips of my fingers, of them sliding when I tried to force them together: an invisible fluid kept them apart. Something invisible but for me fully understandable kept his mouth at a little distance from mine and made his fingers insensitive, stiff and cold.

Then we went to the party. It was full of people, many friends. Not less than three of them were with new wives or husbands. I noticed my husband's expression when he looked at those happy people whose separation was behind them (again the Scottish terrier) and who were united anew, happily snout to snout.

Those thoughts made me dance more wildly and chatter more nonsense than usual. Finally I found myself sitting with my elbow against an old friend's elbow, and to a woman I didn't know I said, apropos my marriage: I am sharing him with another! And she, that wonderful, sensitive, thinking, intelligent being exclaimed: How painful!

That, I really appreciated. I would never forget her. Then the party broke up, we went home and fell asleep back to back, without magnetism but with a definitely friendly feeling between us:

a sort of sensitivity of the skin, a benevolent layer where something could possibly germinate if it came flying. But the only thing that flew in were some mosquitoes and a moth.

When I woke up I found the moth crushed, a velvety mass under my cheek. I sat up and thought about the fact that yesterday had been the day I was supposed to begin my studies in philosophy. I swallowed the tears that always came when I thought about the fact that today was a new day in a new, and for me, incomprehensible period in my life. Then I understood that my studies in philosophy had actually been taking place for a long time. The question was only whether I would ever pass the exam.

On The Way Home

March is annoying. Heat that turns the snow to slush at mid-day. Then, toward evening, a cutting wind sweeps the road. Ruts freeze and crunch when you walk on them. When he reaches the bend he turns around, because he thinks he has heard a black-bird. But the landscape is quiet. Completely silent. One single win-dow is lit at the country store. He was the last customer. The wife stood there rubbing her hands. Nervous about her dinner already cooking on the stove. There was a good smell coming from the kitchen. The girls from Stockholm were leaving just as he arrived. They were talking about pancakes and pork. "You're supposed to cook that on an open fire, girls!" he told them grinning his widest grin. "But are you supposed to use smoked or salt. . .?" "Well. . ." suddenly he didn't know. "Smoked of course," he said with great self-assurance, but then covered what he said with another big smile. Just in case it was wrong.

The girls' house is hidden behind trees. There is only the store-keeper's gable window like a yellow postage stamp. Then the plain to the left, now that he's turned around again, and the woods to the right. But he does hear something after all: it is the constant small wind that sifts through the frozen stubble-field and makes last year's cow parsley rustle on the banks of the ditches.

Straight up the sky is deep blue. He bends his neck until his hair touches the leather collar of his coat and his hat starts sliding off backwards. His arms twitch to stop it. But he is holding a paper bag decorated with "Lyx-Extra, Luxury Coffee for every day" in each hand. The bags are filled with cans, packages of milk, butter, paper towels. And yes, also coffee. Of the "Luxury" sort. He hasn't got a free hand to hinder his hat's maneuvres. So he straightens up again. But there are stars in his eyes. And there, at the horizon, between the store and the spruce forest, where the deciduous trees form a thin palisade, there is an unusually bright one. The evening star.

Then, when he straightens up and starts off again he sees only black. He walks east, then northeast. Toward night and the forest.

He doesn't hurry. And yet he makes good time. His strides swallow the distance. "Why don't you take your bicycle?" Ellen asked when he left. "Do you think that would get me there faster?" He wanted to know. All she could do to answer was roll up her eyes. A while later the gate slammed shut, and he slipped away with springy steps. His boots bend softly. Toes up. Heel on the ground. And yet he doesn't make any noise. He walks as though in stocking feet, even now on frozen ground with his heaviest winter boots, iron-bound both at the toes and the heels. Only once in a while can you hear a crunching under his feet, as though he had stepped on half solidified caramel batter. That's when the thin ice in the ruts cracks a little in order to solidify again when the moon rises and it gets seriously cold.

Soon he can hear the brook. It has a new sound now that the muffling effect of the snow is gone. That happened last week when there was both sunshine and wind. Since then the brook has babbled and gurgled. On Sunday he'll take Ellen along to look for colts-foot. If she is in the mood.

Rapids Forest they call this part of the country. A crazy man from Uppsala kept sheep here one summer. He can't help smiling into the March evening when he remembers the lanky man always with his pipe and a striped silk tie like people in show business. He blabbered about sheep until he was blue in the face. But it didn't do the sheep any good. They wasted away and died. The man disappeared long before the vet slaughtered the last of them because of some plague that hit them. Somebody saw his picture on a T.V. program. That was a year later. "See! That's the sort he was. Academic. Full of hot air. To come here and think he knows all about sheep. . . well, I never! As though you could put sheep out to pasture in Rapids Forest!" "Yes but. . ." the storekeeper down in the village wondered. "I don't think it was such a silly idea." That one. He'd defend anybody. He was nice. You had to give him that. A nice guy. But the man from Uppsala, he was just plain stupid.

A stone rolls and lands in front of his toes. He kicks it for a ride. Maybe it has been rolling for a long time. Propelled by sleds. Under the wheels of cars. Further back maybe it got a ride with the inland ice. Perhaps it came from the North Pole? Now it gets to roll eight, ten meters from one single kick. Most likely it is surprised if it is capable of such.

He stops and looks for it in the dusking light. Is that it there? Grey, with black eyes, like a small potato? Because it certainly wasn't that pale one there which looks so nice that he would bend down to pick it up if it weren't for the bags. That one looks as though it could shine in the dark. Maybe made of that stuff called uranium. Or, rather, quartz, of course. So nice and white and smooth. Guess it got here with the gravel truck last winter when they sanded the roads.

No, he thinks to himself, as his boots start off again. If you start picking up stones, you never know what it'll lead to. There was a sort of half-wit who used to live in the shack. That was a long time ago now. Let's see. Off hand he'd say fifteen years ago. But when you start thinking. . .Ellen and he have been living in The Birches for twenty years already. My God. "Time flies!" as the parson's wife always used to say when she wanted to excuse herself for not having invited them for midsummer coffee. And at that point it was usually September, even October already. "Time does fly, doesn't it!"

And before that they had occupied Lillbacken. For a good five years. But that was five years too many. A lousy rat hole. But The Birches is getting to be elegant now. Since the kids are out in the world. Lisbet and Bruno. Already grown and self-supporting. So, now they could afford making improvements. New linoleum. The bathroom. A washing machine. Great fun! "Out of my way, ol' woman, here comes the machine operator," he hollers. And Ellen can just sit around and do nothing. But that she's got to do by herself. It was just awful when the water leaked in under his sleeves when he stood with his hands over his head and those damn little clothes pins and the sheets, wet and heavy that blew all over his face. But the worst thing was the water running up inside his sleeves. It felt awful. "Roll up your sleeves, you silly man!" But he'd just walk into the living room. Turn on the radio so as not to hear her grinning, he said.

But actually, he loves it. That is her laughing. Oh, how he longs for it when she has her silent days. Sanitary napkins! Oh, yes, he remembered them. In the beginning when they first got married, he never wanted to buy her things like that. But then when she got polio, it suddenly became a matter of course. And not just that. But a lot more having to do with her body. It sounded crazy, but in some way he was happy about those sick years. Naturally, only because it ended well and she got her health back, of course. No one could see anything. But she used to say that her left foot got sort of tired at times.

He was happy about that time, because it felt good to be allowed to wash her whole body. And whatever modesty she had felt about his fingers touching her and feeling inside of her, disappeared when he could be of use in that way. And he himself enjoyed it without shame. And she, as well, liked it too. And her head! How good it felt in his hands when her black hair was slippery and full of soap and lay there like a sort of fine-mesh fabric beneath his hands. He knew every single seam of her skull and the hollow in the back that got filled with a sea of sweat whenever she made a big effort.

And all he learned about the kitchen those years! "Fixing food is fun," he used to say to his friends in the shooting club. That made some of them angry. They felt provoked. But the kids complimented him and said that his meatballs were better than mom's. "You're getting to be just like another girlfriend," Ellen used to say when they sat discussing recipes in the women's magazines. That made him wonder whether she disliked him that way. But when he considered going a step further and ask whether he had become sort of too unmanly for her, he saw the twinkle in her eyes and his whole body felt how superfluous such a question was.

Lisbet. She would pick the stone up anyway he was thinking. She wouldn't pay attention to what he told her about what happened to that crazy guy who lived in the shack. "Do you remember what it was like when you were little at Lillbacken?" he said to her last time she was home on vacation. "We used to take walks on the lane that leads from the big road to Woodcastle. It was a strange lane, because the lake reached all the way up to the roots of the trees on one side. And on the other, the hillside went straight up like a wall. But the trees were beautiful and old. And, way up, lying in the forks of the branches, there were great big smooth stones. Not in every one of them, perhaps. But here and there."

Lisbet remembered, she said. "There was that poor guy who lived in the shack, right?" Just like Ellen. Poor guy! But she had been very relieved anyway when he was put into a home. Because suddenly it was so awfully dark and there were rats and snakes out and God knows what whenever she was supposed to go out to get the milk on autumn evenings. And the reason most likely was that their storage place was near the path that lead to his shack! It hadn't been hard to figure that out. So he used to go with her. For the sake of keeping the peace.

But how on earth had he done it? Had he walked around there at night, since no one ever saw him in daytime, with a long ladder that he put up against the trees? And what about the stones? After all, they were big as heads of babies, sometimes. Smooth and round. Where had he found them? And how did he manage carrying them while climbing up the ladder? Perhaps in a backpack. What a sight if anyone had seen him. But nobody did. When daylight came people just said: "Look, now there's a stone on *that* branch too. It certainly wasn't there the day before yesterday. Because that's when I took a walk here and thought I'd check on how many stones he'd put up, the nitwit." That's what people said.

Like somebody laid them there. A stone bird. From the Stone Age maybe? In the Sunday paper he had read a story about how the earth had cracked and from the crevice came sauropoda and dinosaurs and all that sort of animals from the warm era. But, of course, that had just been a made-up story.

They put him in a home. And he wanted to take along an enormous bag. From under his bed. When he died they opened it and it was full of stones. Big ones and little ones. All of them smooth and round. Some of them as big as cabbages. Others like pigeon eggs.

That's the real truth.

Suddenly it is lighter again. His boots have turned off to the left into the last stretch home. It has all been automatic. Or maybe, out of the corner of his eyes he has registered: the unused milk stand, silver grey, paint peeling; the blue mailbox with their name and number; the silhouette of the old homestead which is a luxury summer cottage now for some foreigner. T.V. aerial on top and a swimming pool in back. And very close to the mailbox, the deeper wheel tracks on his own road, with less space between the ditches. A very humble meeting with the country road: a tributary of gravel winding across the meadow.

There's a field here, you see. That's why it is lighter. The old homestead lies as though on an island in the middle of the field. And it was an island once upon a time. Then, after only half a kilometer, the small road has had its fill of field and open sky and slinks off into the woods like a scared garter snake. But at that point there's only a couple minutes walk left. Hardly more than a curtain of spruce to protect the house from view. Then there are new fields, and those are his own. There are birches surrounding the house, that's where the name comes from. And the plot itself, with its fruit trees, and kitchen garden and lawn where Bonso runs back and forth on his leash, the whole plot backs onto the spruce curtain somehow. The road leads to the side of the house. The door they use most is the one in the gable.

He sniffs the air to see whether he can smell the smoke from the stove. Once he smelled fried onions all the way down on the country road. But this time he can only smell the cold. He thinks: frost. Then he sees the house and the windows. And the sky, velvet blue with a few ragged reddish clouds in the west, is reflected in the windows. Apparently she hasn't lit the lamps. And is unhappy again. Even though she was so cheerful all of last year.

That's what is going through his head, very rapidly, when she suddenly appears from behind the lilac bushes, startling him, and stands right in front of him.

"What on earth!" You can hear his heart beating. Maybe that's why he bursts out laughing so loudly, "Have you started to jump out of bushes like a cat!"

But her face is so white and her eyes are so red that his laughter stops short. Cools down in the March wind to an icy smile and he licks nervously around in his mouth and feels his saliva cover his lips like cool coins. And he doesn't dare ask.

She throws her arms around him and sobs. "It's Lisbet. Bruno called. She tried... She tried to kill herself."

"Do they know. . ." He is so hoarse he has to try again. "Do they know whether she will live?"

"No, goddammit!" And now she is screaming so loud that there is an echo between the house and the chicken coop and the black wall of spruces. "No, they don't know anything yet, and it can take hours! Oh my God! Gustav! Put your arms around me, hold me tight. I think I'm going crazy!"

He puts his arms around her and is unaware that his bags fall to the ground and that in one of them something breaks. And the pain makes him wild and he moves his grip from her shoulders to her waist and hardly knows whether he is comforting or just lusting for her. And they stand there as though they were one single human being. A lamentation for two voices emanates from their two-figured body.

There's a snapping in the woods. Then the rumble of the Stockholm train like long, far away thunder. And afterwards an unbelievable silence.

He has picked up the bags and carries both in one hand even though it is a strain on the paper handles. With the other arm he half carries, half drags Ellen. They progress very slowly toward the side door which she had left open when she ran out to meet him. Or, has she possibly been out here waiting for a long time? In nothing but her flimsy dress?

He walks slowly, shuffling like an old man. The bags in one hand. Ellen under the other arm. Two such great weights. He can't understand that he is so weak. He puts his feet down carefully, one in front of the other. When he walked here an hour ago, it was on gravel which lay on firm ground, a part of the earth. Now he walks on a crust of thin ice. Darkness can swallow them any time. The only part of him that feels alive is his right hand which is digging hard into her waist so as to get a better grip. It seeks comfort in her warmth like a little animal. And his eyes skim the roof and the apple trees, understanding nothing.

Something in the bag is surely broken, he thinks.

Then they arrive at the door.

Mrs. Jenkin's
Wonderful Journey

"This is sure going to be a wonderful trip," I can hear her chirping behind me in the line. Wonderful, she's been chattering about it all morning long. But it's such a warm day, and in the middle of summer too.

"What's one supposed to take a trip for anyway?" I say, and look at her hard. But of course, she just gives me that smile of hers and looks away toward the bus stop, where there's nothing but gravel and strange clocks that look like boxing gloves, except one that's naked, and tells the time without being ashamed. Otherwise it's just gravel, and gravel, and more gravel.

"Gravel and people. Is that something worth seeing?"

But she's satisfied with just about anything, poor thing. Pretty shabbily dressed, she is, too, but that's all right for this sort of a gravel outing, I guess.

"Gravel outing!" I say out loud, to once and for all get her to consider the problem. But she's so wishy-washy, you can tell her just about anything. She'll agree no matter what. Like right now, she's trying to explain that as soon as the bus comes, everything'll be different. I can just imagine: a big ugly bus in the middle of this dreary gravel square, that's going to be different, all right! There it comes already now: yellow enamel with green edges. Boy! We're all going to cook together in there, all day long. So that's what it's like to take a trip. I think I have to laugh out loud. Ha, haha, hahaha...hahahahaha!!

It's going to be hot. I knew it already this morning. Very hot and uncomfortable, and completely unnecessary. What do we have to take this trip for? Can you tell me that?

"What's it good for anyway—can you give me an answer to that?"

Despite my just asking casually in a friendly tone of conversation, the little woman gets all embarrassed and looks at the people sitting around us in the bus, with a stupid smile. As though we had any connection with them! And the sun attacks the tin roof, and on top of it all, they've cut out a hole, so that the sun can fry us to a crisp even better.

Now she's been talking constantly for a long while, and I've politely put in little yes-I-see's and is-that-so's, so that she'll be satisfied and stop talking sometime. You'd really think that she could at least spare me her stupidity, since I'm doing what she wants, taking the trip.

"It sure is getting warm, isn't it, my dear," I say lightly putting her off—you have to keep her at a distance—and then I devote myself to looking out of the window. It is awfully dusty, but I can still see all the green we're driving through. Bushes and trees and fields. I can make it all out very well. And after I've looked at it all for over an hour, I say to her—and this time I really want an answer:

"But what exactly is the purpose of all this? Green and green, nothing but green trees, and bushes and fields. I've seen it all now, so for my sake we don't have to go any further!"

That gets her started on Jones' Island again. And what is Jones' Island? An island. And there's nothing green on it? Of course there is, it is all beautifully green. It is nice to look at all this green, she says, for city eyes.

"Do you have city eyes?" I say harshly, and turn away. I don't understand anything at all. She could at least let me know what all of this is supposed to be good for...I've seen it now, her be-au-ti-ful green.

"It is a strange journey anyway," I say. "Just trees and trees. What about Jones' Island? Are we going to be there soon?"

"No, first we have to cross the water," she says, "and then we'll be on Jones' Island."

"And then?"

"Then, well..."

Only evasive replies to everything. Never an honest answer. As though just traveling were enough! The wonderful journey she's been talking about for such a long time: sitting on this unusually ugly-colored plush seat with steel handles at the back and facing the back of a woman's neck with ratty hair and a red pimple, and then to the left, the tip of a little woman's nose. To the right only green trees and bushes. Which are green, too! "It is a strange journey, don't you agree? I mean, just sitting here and looking at all the green!"

But no one else seems to wonder. They sit there like mushrooms, grown fast to their mossy plush seats, and from time to time sly smirks pass over their faces, as though they knew something. Something secret, of course! Why don't I ever get to know anything!

"But then, on Jones' Island," I say to the little woman next to me, "what are we going to do there?"

"Oh, it's going to be so nice there," she answers. (Nice? What does that mean?) "Delightful and green. We'll take a walk in the green and then we'll get coffee at the Home, and then we'll go back on the evening bus, as you know."

Go back! My God! Do we have to go back the same way!

"Do you mean that we're sitting here just so that we can do the whole thing all over again backwards! No, in that case I think I'd rather get off right away. It can hardly get any greener than this."

But the little being in her shabby suit looks scared and upset when I say that, so I just sit where I am, because otherwise one never knows what she might do.

I'm already sweaty under my hat. I knew it would be warm. People who take this sort of trip must be terribly cold natured.

"A strange journey! Isn't it?" I say to the young man diagonally in front of me and give him a friendly pat on the back. The neck of the woman to his right turns red under her straggly hair. I see, jealous of course. Oh, people are...

"Pardon me?" says the rosy cheeked one, and turns around to see who he is talking to. He is a friendly, well-brought up young man who knows how to behave. You can tell right away. I'm sure he can tell me what this is all about. The little woman is a silly goose.

"Well, I think it is so strange, to just sit here and ride!"

Now I'm aware that people around me are giggling and getting very silly. Haven't these people been taught any manners?

"Don't you think, sir, that it is very strange to travel in this way, through all that green. It's an outing, my little traveling companion here says. But I do think it's rather a strange outing..."

"Well, it's fast of course," he says gravely. "And that is sort of strange in a way."

That, I don't agree with! Fast! This?

"No, I think the gentleman is really wrong there. It certainly isn't fast, as you say, but so extremely green! And what is it all good for in the end?"

For, despite the fact that our opinions differ so much, I realize immediately that he is a worthy interlocutor, someone more reasonable than my little woman companion.

"What it's good for?" he says, tasting the words. That gave him something to think about!

"Isn't it sort of nice to get out to the country, where you can see summer from close up?"

"Oh, summer!" I retort. "Do you think, sir, that you can see summer? From close up? Perhaps behind all the green, but this bus drives so carefully through it all, that you'd think it was theatre scenery." You'd have to get out into the green, and then perhaps...But in reality, I doubt that you can see the summer.

"And what does one see, sir? ...the backs of people's necks, and people who smirk. A driver, who drives. And you know, it's so awfully irritating..."

"What do you mean irritating?...I don't understand..."

"I mean my corset. It chafes me because it doesn't move together with my body. My skin is all irritated from the heat, you see. Here, feel! It actually smells like burning rubber! And this is what they call a nice outing. A real nice outing, I must say! Ha!"

It is so quiet, suddenly. I listen and it seems that even the motor has stopped. Of course they're all pretty seedy people, but I still don't want them to get any insight into my private life, and then use it in all sorts of inappropriate ways. And I sure don't intend to be subject matter for some conversation between country yokels!

No, the motor's still rumbling. That's, of course, because the speed makes it go round just like the wheels. And that man in front in the driver's uniform, I wonder if he's a real driver? Attached, as he is, to his big wheel, he has to push buttons and pull levers all at the same time. That they still have that kind of punishment. Sometimes he peeks at us in the little mirror and just sees us indistinctly, but some day he will see us clearly like when a sail is lowered and the silver ball itself is seen rolling cool and smooth over the waves.

"Really an unusual journey, my dear!" I say. At that she suddenly picks up her knitting and her oranges and whispers—very loudly—that now she's sick and tired of all my questions, and she'll move to the back of the bus to get some peace and quiet!

"Don't forget to let me know when we're supposed to get off," I shout amiably after her. After all, she is so unaware of things.

I almost sighed with relief when I carefully spread myself out over the two seats.

"Do you know where we are now?" I wonder cheerfully and the charming young man turns around with a smile.

"I don't really know what this place is called."

"How strange! You travel some place you don't know what it's called or where it is. That's really strange."

"You don't seem to be enjoying this trip," he says.

Trip! I have to laugh. We've all been taken in, taken for a trip, a real trip-up, ha, ha!

"And at the end of the road, is that where you get off?" he wants to know.

"No, on Jones' Island," I inform him. "We're getting off on Jones'

Island, me and my little friend," I tell him, and I point to her there furthest back in the bus where she is sitting surely as a bear with a sore head.

"Jones' Island," says the man. "That's where the road ends. The whole island ends there. The last stop on Jones' Island is called Jones' Island," he explains. "But, of course, there are more islands out there."

Exactly! More and more islands out there. And they're just as green, and then there are more islands that are even greener. And buses with people in them who say that it is warm and that they've arrived now although anyone who has the energy to stay put knows that they've only come half way so far. That's exactly what I mean!

"But don't worry so much about it," the young man says gravely. (I think he's a priest.) "Don't think so much about it now, it's a long way yet."

"Aha, I bet you're a priest," I say, and thump him triumphantly in his black back. "Don't think so much! That's where you gave yourself away, my good man!"

I'm aware suddenly of a kind of bustle around us—as though all that green had come and invaded the bus and was whisking around with its branches and leaves and sending out its titillating smells. It is laughter! All around me the whole bus is laughing.

But the man in black turns away and looks hurt, even his back looks offended.

"Has the gentleman been to Jones' Island?" I continue unperturbed to let him know that I'm not the sort that holds a grudge.

"We're there now," he says rather sullenly and to my great surprise.

"So this is Jones' Island! But we haven't crossed any water yet," I say jokingly.

"Yes we have. Twenty minutes ago." He still looks unhappy, like a school boy with warts on the bottom of his feet.

"Now you're making fun of me, my good man," I say. Perhaps he wants to be addressed as "Sir" or "Pastor" but I don't give a damn about that. After all, does anyone address me according to my position?

"It is a very small body of water, lady," a woman on the other side of the aisle says suddenly.

"Thank you so much for the information," I say and smile graciously. But I think they're making a fool of me!

"Did you hear that this is supposed to be Jones' Island, my friend?" I shout to the back of the bus.

"Just sit still, Mrs. Jenkins, we're soon getting off," the little goose answers. As though I'd said something entirely different! She's really behaving very strangely, the little thing. From time to time I really wonder about her common sense!

"But where's the water?" I wonder. "If this is an island"—they must all be aware of the ironic doubting tone in my voice—"if this is an island, then it's only logical that there should be water."

"It is a very large island," says my priestly friend.

A very large island! Smart, ha? That way you can explain away just about everything in the world! The island is so big, you can't see the water! The island is so little, you can't see anything but water! Haha! It's such a little mainland, people call it an island, no? Hahaha. How can they expect one to trust that sort of information? So this green is supposed to be Jones' Island as opposed to the exact same green we drove through twenty minutes ago?

"Excuse me, sir," I begin extremely politely. I always try to behave courteously even when dealing with common people. "But I wonder, what is the name of the area we've just driven through, that is, before we reached this so-called Jones' Island?"

He clears his throat and looks rather embarrassed. "As a matter of fact," he begins hesitatingly, "that is called Jones' Island as well, although it actually is part of the mainland."

Is that so! That's called Jones' Island! And this is called Jones' Island. Why then, did we go to Jones' Island, when we already were on Jones' Island? Can somebody explain that for me? Or do they take me for an idiot?

But out loud I am very diplomatic—you have to be diplomatic with this sort of stupid people:

"I see. Jones' Island. And Jones' Island. Green and green. No water there. No water here. But still, an island here and mainland there!" And I add deploringly:

"It must be extremely difficult to keep these things apart. But I have come to realize that you are very intelligent." (And despite the fact that I don't mean to, I say those last words in an ironical tone, which makes him sink down in his seat.)

"And so you can perhaps also explain to me what the object is in driving through these waterless islands and meadows in this dusty sweaty pressure cooker?"

To think that she's fooled me into taking this horrible trip just to irritate me. And all these people laugh constantly. Is that the price they pay for their existence? And what about me? All of this indecision: is it an island, or isn't it an island? Is it a meadow or a beach? Is it the front or the back? Is it summer or theatre scenery?

Not a decent answer have I received all this time. Here I sit in a corset and silk blouse, a flowery suit and high heeled nurse's shoes and with my hat squeezed down on my wet forehead. Sweat is running down my back inside the girdle. But despite it all, I'm terribly strong. When I tighten my muscles I can hear the plush seat creak, and I see sparks when I make a fist.

And me, they can't give an answer to?

Haha!

I must have sighed loudly because now they all turn around and giggle, the stupid busybodies. But I haven't said anything at all. I just sit here in this bus and look through a very dusty window, and see all the green go by backwards at great speed and sometimes it all stops and becomes trees and is quiet and then it starts moving all over again, as though someone were standing there pulling an enormous green tablecloth off an immense table.

I know how to behave. I watch them and do as they do. I sit quietly and look out as though I were interested in their green, as though the whole journey were something completely natural, well motivated, thoroughly thought out and carefully planned.

Most likely they don't know anything themselves. No, probably it's like this: they're not hiding anything from me because they don't have anything to hide. I bet.

"A strange journey, don't you think?" I say in a friendly tone to the woman with the pointed nose across the aisle. People usually enjoy it when I converse with them a little. "Just grass and trees, and still this is supposed to be the famous Jones' Island. We're on an outing there now, but the whole thing is really rather strange. Don't you think so too?"

But nobody thinks that it is strange. And the bus keeps on rolling through its tunnel of road dust and sun.

On Distance Between People

A bullfinch fell like a frozen apple. Straight down into the snow, she thought, but that was most likely only what it looked like.

Whenever she stood there, for a long time, watching the snow falling, the curtains and the window frames seemed to move upward. And, when she stood there for too long, her back began to ache. Therefore, she straightened up, passed her hand over the arm rest of the kitchen sofa, a habit, as though to clean, sweep up, smooth out. She cupped her left hand as though she expected to find crumbs. Then she stroked the sides of her body and her thighs vigorously. No one else ever did.

Her feet tangled in the rag rug. The old fringes were frayed and lay against the linoleum floor like wisps of grey hair. You should hem the carpet instead, her daughter always admonished. Make a selvage. Reinforce it with binding tape. She would nod vigorously so that they would stop having to talk about it. Her fingers remembered very well the last time she tried to mend a rug. It was the big one from the dining room, the one with blue stripes. The needle was long and thick. The thread got caught, and she pulled and pulled at it. Then when she pushed the needle into the thick resisting fabric, the old thimble cracked, and the eye of the needle, together with the thread, penetrated into the fleshy cushion of her middle finger, got stuck there and had to be pulled out.

Her fingers remembered many things in the house. They were intimately acquainted with most things. She would be able to manage even if she should lose her sight, she had thought when she had to exchange her glasses for stronger ones. Her fingers could find their way. They knew every surface, every crack. Even the space behind the kitchen stove, where, when she pulled it one day she found remains of food—cereal that had cooked over, dead twigs of juniper, rat poison and the neat little skeleton of a shrew, nibbled clean by the black death-watch beetles which came gravely out of nooks and crannies, their backs covered with dust.

For a long time she had kept the little skeleton lying on her sewing box in the hall next to the kitchen. Then it had disappeared. Perhaps after a visit from her daughter. Her daughter cleaned and put things in order, sometimes too much in order. In the beginning she cried when she lost something: there was so little, after all, that she could call her own. Then, slowly, she understood how important it was for the girl, this orderliness, how it had to do with her very being and her profession, for that matter. She designed patterns for textiles: straight lines, clear colors. Therefore, she considered all that was discarded, hidden or stored away to be unnecessary ballast, something that must be thrown out of the sled, to the wolves, so as to escape safe and sound, she and her daughter. And her husband. She couldn't really visualize him in the sled, perhaps because he was so large. He didn't really fit. Or perhaps because he would have ridiculed that sort of thinking, about riding in a sled and having to throw things out to the wolves. He would be just contemptuous as he had been the time she told him she had been asked to sing in the church choir. "What are you going to stand there and bawl for?" he wanted to know disagreeably. "Don't you have anything else to do, and besides, the roads are dark and slippery. Just as well you stay home."

And so he put distrust, guilt, fear, and a vague feeling of concern about her into one single sentence. She had to sit down. Automatically she reached for the telephone, but he misinterpreted the movement and said in a mollifying tone: "You don't have to say no right away. Think it over first."

He didn't know that she used to phone Lisbet, her old classmate in the next town, when things were really difficult. Or, when they were good: like on the day when the riding school from down in the village galloped across the snowy fields in the sunshine, the horses' hooves kicking up plumes of sparkling snow, their hind quarters glistening, their breath like smoke and the hunting dogs down at the surveyor's starting to bark. It's like a piece of tapestry, you know, she shouted into the telephone, and the words gushed out, because Lisbet simply had to see the brilliant spectacle she was seeing.

She certainly was needed. How could they manage otherwise? Mother should have more help in the household, her son said when he visited on weekends, sometimes by himself, sometimes with his wife and baby. Her daughter didn't say that; she helped instead. Her son had white smooth hands just like his father. Even though he was a librarian, a rather dusty profession. Book dust and printer's ink. But it was as though it didn't fasten in the same way as stove blacking, scouring powder, soil and grease. Mother should wear rubber gloves, he also used to say, putting her hand to his cheek. And her daughter gave her a pair of gardening gloves.

"But I want to feel the roots. My fingers have to know what they're doing down there," she said to justify herself. They want to know whether there is a stone, or a worm, whether it is a shoot on the root of the ash tree, that has to be removed, or the dahlia bulb that has to be taken up unharmed.

Even on the day her fingers closed hard around a piece of glass and she had to take a taxi to the clinic and get a tetanus shot, she told her daughter on the telephone that it felt better without gloves. "I like to feel the soil," she said. "But..." her daughter tried. "That's the way I am," she said then.

Sometimes she wondered about the tendency of dirt to stick together, its solidarity with other dirt, the surface tension around the kitchen tap where it always accumulated. She must speak to her son-in-law about this. He was an astronomer and often talked about how matter clustered together in the universe, how freely-floating atoms actually seem to search restlessly across space for others like them, in need of friction and heat.

That's the way it was with crumbs, collections of moisture, burned off matches, extremely small bits of Christmas ham, red cabbage, orange peel. All of it congregating, merging together with a couple of drops of coffee, a splash of beer, a few grains of salt. Suddenly it was a little world, a meeting place. Preferably just there, around the tap. She rubbed it away gently with the fingertips of both hands. For a moment the stainless steel shone softly and brightly toward her. But when she turned around to take the rag rug out, something turned up, something fell down from the ceiling or came sailing on the wings of a fly.

As soon as she came out the birds came flocking. Even what was shaken off the rug was good enough to eat. The bullfinches enticed each other with melancholy calls, the titmice scratched and chattered like miniature magpies. She went in to get the ball of tallow in its net of yarn. Soon she had hung it and it swung like a pendulum. The big magpie came flying, staggered and swayed, bumped into the apple-tree, and behaved clumsily, something animals seldom do. After a short while she had enough and surrendered the nourishing ball to the onslaught of nuthatches and blue tits.

While she reported on the life in the apple tree her husband turned pages in his book, with his long white fingers. From time to time he glanced up over his glasses, as though to see her, but she knew that was his blind spot. When he wanted to know something of importance like "Where is my shirt?" or "Are we going to have dinner sometime today?" he would look at her directly, through his glasses. When he pushed them up he was blind and unreachable. He held the book in front of his face like a shield.

She bent down over the sink. A tea-brown substance had settled around the small holes over the drain. She rubbed it with her thumbnail, then with a scouring pad and cleanser.

She straightened up and listened. The house was abnormally silent. It could only mean that the washing machine had stopped: it was the interval between washing and drying. She lifted out all of the tangled, clean clothes. A heavy lump even though spin-dried.

Carefully, she separated his pale, long underwear from the pink twin cups of her brassiere. Stockings were tangled in snares and figure eights around the white sail of her apron and the sprawling flower design of his Sunday shirt. A couple of bedsocks fell out like wet tennis balls and rolled under the stack of firewood. Getting down on her knees with difficulty, she got them out from the dark with the help of the cane. She returned the cane to its place with great care; it had a silver handle and had belonged to her father-in-law. Using it had been tabooed ever since the children were small. No, it had never been used against either of them, but rescuing balls with it from under the sofa, or poking down a ripe apple from the tree, or reaching for a badminton ball in the drain-pipe was absolutely prohibited. And just because of that it was constantly used for all these things, and much more. It had been their secret manifestation of disobedience, an unspoken conspiracy against their father and grandfather, the users of the cane.

Trembling with awe, as though holding a scepter that had belonged to a Bronze Age chieftain, the children used to sneak out with the cane to make holes in the icy surface of the water in the barrel. Like a conspirator, with a laugh that was no more than an inside quiver, she would take the cane down from its hook to remove the spiderwebs that had been woven between the water pipes above the hat shelf. Once she extinguished a candle on a Christmas tree by hitting it with the silver handle. He almost never found out. In any case, she could not remember any greater row or punishment. But it must have happened some time, there must have been a time when someone was judged and sentenced, when a ban was imposed, otherwise, why should they have been so ridiculously afraid?

Even now she replaced the cane very quietly, but it clattered against the cast iron umbrella stand nevertheless. She heard him cough from the upstairs hall where he was sitting and reading.

"Would you like some tea?" she called up, in order to muffle the clatter. He condescended obligingly, saying that perhaps a cup of tea wouldn't be such a bad idea, and she got the tea tray ready. With two cups. Then they sat there a while like husband and wife, and he read aloud out of the newspaper about fraud in the art world of the capital and a massacre in Namibia. Around thirty skeletons of children had been found. She put down her cup. Many of them had been tortured before they were shot. She returned the half-eaten cinnamon bun to her plate. "Do you have to, just when we're eating?"

"Whether we are eating or not makes no difference to them. They're dead, after all. You must learn to differentiate between murder,"—and he assumed a threatening pose, making his fist into a pistol directed at her—"murder, I say, in real life and this,"—he struck the paper dramatically with his hand—"which is words, words, words and nothing more than words!"

"But perhaps we could talk about this later, when..."

"Yes, you tell me. When? Afternoon tea belongs together with newspaper reading. My father taught me that. And I have done it ever since my years at Uppsala. We always read the paper together, the papers, that is, because we had several at that time, me and my first wife."

And at that his eyes unexpectedly became moist, and she stirred her tea solicitously, not daring to look at him. That was the worst: when he did show feelings. That was when she realized that she didn't want to see them.

The snow continued falling. When she went downstairs with the tray she saw dead flies on the window sill and some that were still alive and moving like blue-black spots in front of her eyes, the sort that appear and disappear when you are tired. She refused to kill them, but to let them out was the same thing. If she let them stay in her warm indoors, there would be more and more of them. The speed at which they multiplied was really amazing. They especially seemed to like the African violets, flew out of them every time she watered.

This morning her daughter had phoned. Yes, she would come, as usual; she only wanted to say, to prepare mother, that she had left home.

Her head swam for a moment, as she stood with the receiver pressed hard against her ear. Left? But hadn't she left home already? It must have been twenty years ago. That was when she was at school and...Yes, of course, she meant her own home. She felt a pang in her stomach as though she had been stabbed with a knife. She had left Ralf and the children, her three grandchildren... She had to sit down on the chair, on top of all the newspapers and the radio program that was lying there and a letter from the organist who directed the church choir. She sat very unsteadily on the uneven pile of newspapers, slid down one side and sat askew, or was it the room that was sliding.

"I should have said something before," she heard her daughter very far away over the wire that was buzzing and sighing. "But we did keep on hoping that things would be all right."

"Be all right?" It sounded like an operation.

"Yes, that we wouldn't need to do anything so drastic. Ralf is so civilized, after all, you can always talk to him. But then it all went too far... Well, mother, you do know his tendencies, don't you..."

"What? You mean..."

"Yes, this little bit that's unmasculine about him. Mother must know about it, I've talked about it quite often. I've been worried about it. And so I went to see a psychologist, a counselor. Well, mother, to make a long story short, he has become homosexual."

She didn't know what to say in the pause that followed that word, so she sat there and looked, without seeing, out at snow. An unusually fat-bellied fly had landed on its back between the geranium pots, and couldn't turn over.

"That is to say, become and become," her daughter went on in a friendly, explaining voice from far away. "I suppose he's been that way all along. But it's becoming more and more obvious. Well, I can't tell you how awful I think it is to tell mother this, sort of like emptying a garbage pail in the midst of your's and father's idyll, out there."

"But what about the children," she managed to say then. "The grandchildren, my grandchildren."

"Ralf will take care of them for the time being," said her daughter. "I've been living at a hotel for a couple of days..."

"So, you have abandoned them!"

"But, mother, didn't you hear me, it's such a bad connection: I've been living at a hotel for a while, but just yesterday I got a little apartment. It's so nice, completely redecorated, all white and yellow. With real wooden floors and a large, bright room where I can have my drawing board and the smaller of the looms."

She couldn't remember what they said after that. Suddenly she sat there at the kitchen table, dusk was over, darkness had come and silenced the birds. She was hemming the table cloth she had received for Mother's Day from her daughter and her Ralf. He had good taste in fabrics and colors. They always got along so well. He had been such a good friend, her daughter had said, but there was more than that, she was thinking: her grandchildren existed, after all.

The loose Indian fabric ran smoothly between her fingers. The iron thimble with its golden rim gleamed in the lamplight. Up and down, the needle went, then the thread tangled into knots. Something was wrong.

She examined the needle. The needle was the cause. Around its middle there was a band in iridescent colors like when a little gasoline is spilled on rain-wet asphalt. This was the needle that had been used for operations and therefore, it had been passed through a flame to be sterilized. Slivers had swollen in a child's foot, the swelling had to be punctured, and the sliver dug out to the accompaniment of much screaming. Or a hair in an eyebrow had become ingrown. Here and there, throughout the years, a mini-operation had been performed, just here, at the kithen table under the bright light of the lamp.

She considered throwing it into the garbage pail, but the idea of this sharp and unexpected object among the eggshells, coffee grounds and paper towels made her wince. Therefore, she stuck it back into the pincushion, a little to one side, then found another needle of the same thickness and sat for a long time aiming with the uncooperative piece of thread before it finally slid into its narrow eye. She sewed, and tears ran down her cheeks.

In the dining room the war between Iran and Iraq had broken

out. This was followed shortly by two thousand dead in a natural catastrophe, and a refugee family that had been deported from the country, from her country, even though she had wanted them to stay.

She sewed, but her fingers were clumsy and slow. The light was bad. The man had already wondered loudly was there not going to be dinner soon. But the meat was frozen and the fish not bought. He didn't like vegetables; that wasn't real food. So, she pretended not to hear and continued to sew; a tablecloth is never so large as when you hem it.

When she ran out of thread the needle decided to disappear. She got up, shook the fabric and listened for its tap hitting the linoleum floor, but heard nothing. She felt her woolen skirt and patted the upholstered seat behind her. For safety's sake she felt inside the sides of her slippers—could it possibly have wedged itself in there? She found her glasses and examined the surface of the kitchen table; there was nothing shiny there. Then she got down on her knees and felt with both hands across the kitchen floor. They found crumbs and dustballs, unidentifiable mini-objects, unknown micro-worlds that the vacuum cleaner had missed. They found a beer bottlecap, and the safety clasp to the old watch-chain she had looked for. A hard-as-stone meatball that rolled around underneath the china cabinet was quickly caught. But she found no needle.

She sat down again with the uncomfortable feeling that something sharp and dangerous was loose and hiding in her kitchen. Homosexual. She tried the word out. Did that make Ralf different, for her? For the children? She couldn't visualize any other man, only Ralf and her daughter and the children as they were biking to go swimming in the summer and turned around to wave so that their bicycles wobbled, and her heart was in her mouth. One week a family, a relationship, next week: a man who lives with his children and a mother who has "a bright little apartment in white and yellow with real wooden floors, I think I'll buy the beautiful set of china I saw, you remember, mother, and what's more, I don't have to keep on doing housework every day..."

Was there a kitchen, for that matter? And what about the children, didn't she want to tuck them in every night, like before, and wake them every morning? But Ralf had done that, actually.

"Aren't we going to have any dinner at all today?" Now he stood there in the open door and looked at her directly through his glasses. She tried to imagine what she looked like sitting there sewing, a little over seventy with a hint of a moustache, grey-haired and wearing the same cornflower-blue cardigan she had worn for the past ten winters. Not a beautiful sight, exactly, but who would sit here if she left? If she got herself a "bright little apartment in white and yellow" in the village for example? Or in Uppsala? There, they have courses in weaving for pensioners, there she could play the piano without disturbing anyone, there people lived and let you live, and she could breathe the air of freedom—or of loneliness.

After a dinner of soup and pudding, she wanted to talk with her husband, the father, about their daughter and Ralf. But, to her surprise, she felt like laughing instead. Getting a divorce from a homosexual, that, he'd agree, was absolutely necessary. But the very fact that their daughter had such a husband, had chosen such a husband, that someone like Ralf existed at all, would irritate him to such an extent that all of this repressed business about Jews, Negroes, immigrants and artists would surge up in him, and that, she couldn't face listening to that again.

How often had she not avoided conversation topics that would expose him as what he really was?

She got ready to do some ironing, placed the ironing board on top of the kitchen table, with a bath towel in between to protect the painted surface of the table. The light shining outside the window showed that it was still snowing. There would be snow during the night, and it would be hard to shovel the path to the mailbox in the morning. Besides, she hadn't managed to formulate the letter to her daughter that she meant to put there.

She suddenly felt as though her husband was made of snow, that she had kneaded and molded him, altered here, dug out there, added a bit and removed another. Then she had pushed a hat down over his ice head and left him to stand there to freeze fast.

But something was wrong, nevertheless. So she had made changes, placed her warm hand on him and he had melted in tears.

Who was he really? And was it so that he was able to live and go through life only if she went first and showed the way? And if so, is that not called manipulating and molding him once more?

"Good night, my friend," he said and interrupted her thoughts. "Are you troubled about something? Are you standing there crying? We'll talk about it tomorrow. Everything always feels easier in the morning." And he patted her cheek, which was unusual. She put her arms around him, and when he took a deep breath to expand his chest, she knew again the well-known feeling of being pushed away, repelled from his heart.

"Good night," she said and sprinkled some more clothes. Just before midnight she opened the kitchen door and breathed in the night air. A sweet-smelling, snowy wind blew through the space between the house and the barn that had been turned into a garage. She took a few steps outside the circle of light and stood kneedeep in new-fallen snow. Everything was enticingly soft and smooth and for a long while she didn't feel the cold; on the contrary, it was though the snow warmed her.

If there were no weather, she was thinking, we would wander in a void. Nothing else shoves us like the wind, or drenches us like the rain, dries us like the sun. Nothing else falls on the roof, starts us shoveling and plowing, makes us hang out the wash or rush it in so that it won't get drenched again. Nothing else wakes us at night pounding on the roof, and makes us pull out television and telephone plugs. Nothing else howls and whistles in the chimney like the most modern of violin concertos.

There are people who talk about the weather constantly, who dare not talk about much else, she thought as she turned the key twice, locking up for the night. Then she turned off the outside lights and went to her room. But, it is really the weather you talk with, it is the long dialogue that lasts from the day of birth until the grave.

No sooner had she formulated the word grave in her mind, than she remembered the accident. When taking out the ironing board to place it on the kitchen table, she had upset one of the old amaryllis bulbs in its pot. They stood in a row in the window near the kitchen door, waiting for the light of spring. The large flowers had wilted, the green leaves hung, yellowed and dry. The one on the left still had its Christmas greeting card tied to it with a piece of golden string: Warm Christmas Greetings from Ralf, it said. It had been his personal Christmas present to her; the rest of the family had given others, more collectively.

That was two months ago. Two months before the little, bright apartment, all in white and yellow and perhaps without a kitchen. What was she going to eat, her girl? Pills?

It had fastened in the metal runner under the ironing board, that card with its golden string, and the pot had fallen over and clumsily rolled down from the sill to land among glass jars and preserving paraphernalia, bucket and empty bottles crowded there on the floor.

She was in her nightgown now and barefoot, but she simply had to go and sweep it up. The soil on the floor felt grainy and powdery under her feet. Where the broom didn't reach she had to use her fingers and a damp rag. There was not only soil on the rag, she noticed when she came into the light of the kitchen, but rat-dung, as well. She washed her hands under the tap and wrote: Attn. rat poison, on a pad.

Then she turned off the light again and sat down on the edge of her bed. Her watch showed that it was a new day already, the day after she was told that a happy family was unhappy. Time rushes by, she thought, soon it will be a year ago, soon the whole thing is forgotten, except in the minds of three grandchildren that are grown by then and different, in some indefinable way, than if it hadn't happened.

He didn't ask for this, she said aloud to her feet as she rubbed mint-scented cream into them. No one is the result of his own creation only, she said to the candle in its glass candle stick, as she lit it on her bedside table.

Then she lay there for a long time and saw the shadows dance on the ceiling when the draft from the window played with the flame. She remembered a friend her son had brought home one summer. He was a philosopher, yes, both academically and in the old-fashioned way, a man who wondered and marvelled and puzzled and orated at the kitchen table late at night. He talked about distance between people, about coolness that was not necessarily coldness. People can live vertically, he said. You have to remember that. The horizontal way of life creates families but also dependencies, societies but also wars. People in crowds wear and tear on each other, can go crazy—like the deer in a zoo, who went insane and started to eat each other.

People can live vertically. Each on his own mountaintop, his sight focused on God or the place in the universe where we imagine Him to be. Like living minarets or totem poles.

There is nothing ugly about that, the young man said, sitting at her kitchen table. There are many ways in which to live; you need to choose a way that causes the least possible damage.

Half asleep, she saw a pair of hands, and they were both her own and her mother's or perhaps her grandmother's, since her mother had died when she was little. They were bony and crippled with rheumatism. She saw them taking hold of a slippery newborn child and pulling, both hard and cautiously. It had to come out to daylight even though it seemed slow and balky.

Now they took hold of long, shiny pieces of gut and stuffed them unevenly with ground meat and then she kneaded and smoothed them out with her fingers so that they became sausages that were tied at regular intervals. Now they pulled cow teats, it must definitely have been grandmother's hands, and the cow teats stretched and let go, but only a little, and shrunk back elastically, but one of them was sore and had to be handled with care, still the milk had to come out, and it drummed against the bottom of the pail but soon the sound was softer and that was when the hands picked up potatoes instead, and they hammered heavy as lumps of clay, and then the sound became duller, little by little, as the pail was filled.

Last they took hold of the man's organ, trembling with solemn solicitude as though it was something holy, then, jovial and impetuous, having fun now, they caressed and kneaded, and they rested with a handful of happiness that no one could see.

Just when she fell asleep, she remembered what it was like when she had slept with a little rill running down her thigh, first warm, then cool and sticky, the stuff people are woven from, she supposed. Or was it only a dream?

The Big Sleep

I'm sitting at the wheel of a car that is crammed with members of my family, the people closest to me: my father, who is ninety-two, my mother in her seventies, two others my age, and the children who are five and eight.

The sun sparkles in from the side where the lakes lie along the Dala River. Its light is intensified and reflected. In the back of the car the youngest two have just made up after a kicking and clawing fight about whose was the juice bottle with the red top, and whose the one with the green top. Now they're sipping out of the same bottle, and whispering that they'll get engaged when they grow up.

The snowy slush on little roads is treacherous. One wrong movement, a sudden collision, and we all lie there in a mess of blood and dirt, intertwined in a new way, shoved together more compactly and decisively than now in this comfortably rocking vehicle. One hundredth of a second of distraction means a catastrophe: broken glass, dented fenders, screams and moans. The silence of death.

The miles rush by. Abandoned ironworks, inlets where people stand fishing, red cottages, white mansions with black roofs. A group of people are having a picnic next to their car. Breath coming smokelike from their mouths, they crack hard boiled eggs against the bumper. Sweden rushes by. Peaceful and sunny on this Sunday in late February. But one single second of drowsiness, of half sleep, and it all becomes a catastrophic madness.

What I'm thinking about is war. Even though the panorama all around me suggests very different thoughts, it is war that occupies the space behind my eyes: it is like a sluggish wild animal, swifter than we think, and it doesn't seem dangerous simply because it has not yet chosen us as its prey.

Actually, I say to myself, there is only one thing to fight against in our world, and that is war. Inside we all know this. But we keep forgetting. We dream a dream of a millenium of peace. We think we've been forgotten up here near the pole. We keep hoping for a new sense of reason in our politicians, a new appreciation of human dignity in those who have the power. Nonsense. It is all fantasy and without foundation. No strategies have helped yet. No politicians have been smart enough. No geographic location has, in the long run, kept a single population safe. Not from war, at least. Not from THIS war.

There are always willing forces on the side of war. There is constant mobilization. People everywhere, men and women like you and me, choose war for their profession, destruction for their craft, bombs and missiles for their industry, while saying, perhaps, that they hope the products of their common endeavors will remain unused.

The only thing that can save us is total awareness. And a common front. Only that, plus an ever-alert conscience, and an increased consciousness, could possibly save us from the next war.

And so, what do we do? We dream...we drive at 70 km an hour along snowy roads where the sun sparkles, we crack our picnic eggs and caress the hair of our loved ones. We talk.

"Whose sister-in-law? Which funeral? And then what'd he say? Actually, culture criticism is a bluff. Who's supposed to be sitting in the academy? What do you mean academy? I said Arcady. So, who's supposed to be in Arcady? What poet lied like he did? I hate soccer. Herring is so expensive now. The way things are at this point, you simply have to invest in trendy gadgets, no matter how ugly they are. There's got to be a cheap supermarket brand beer glass on every dinner table. And they last forever. Who would have thought that there would be frost in the middle of the blooming period? Not an apple, not a single one, I said. You don't have to believe me...But there were lots of mountain ash berries at any rate."

And the cloud that can be seen hovering over Lake Grycken is not one of those storm clouds that flyers fear; it is instead the ashes of war. We cannot hear it as yet, but it hangs like a threat over us all.

You don't burn yourself voluntarily with a candle. You don't deliberately stick a darning needle into your thumb. You don't drink gasoline instead of champagne. But we do watch the approach of the future war and shrug our shoulders. From time to time we become aware of our nightmare—as though we were waking out of anaesthesia: when we find an old gas mask in the attic, discover steps down to a shelter among the rose bushes in the park, or see an unusually threatening headline. Afterwards it's all erased again. Like a dream. We rub our eyes, and what do we see: Sweden. Sweden, our native land, hot dogs, the first day of school, circus posters, television reruns, bargain sales, unemployed teenagers, persistent low pressure weather, sleeping M.P.'s—although no longer so much in the chambers because of the advent of television.

Sleep of one single second and we're all a bloody mess. I wish I had something else to say, like: a sleep of one single second, and we all feel rested, as though we had spent time on a cloud and were now happily embarking on the second half of our journey, our journey home. But statistics point to other things.

The worst thing is that I think I know I will never write about it. Why? Because the present is so beautiful? No, it's not that simple.

It is because I don't use the right rousing sort of words. I don't know the statistics. I don't have the vocabulary. Because I'm an amateur in politics. And because the character of the world is such that war and people have belonged together for hundreds of thousands of years. Who am I then to be so frightened, frightened enough to scream?

I'm so terribly afraid of that war that words fail me. Can I hide behind this fact? I think that I would prefer sleeping a while, just a little while in a curve between Moklinta and Runhallen. . .The gravel squeaks, the heavy vehicle shakes. Everything depends upon how well I coordinate the movements of my right and left arms with what I see and what I know. Within the fragile walls of our car sit those defenseless people whom I love most in the world. A couple of them are young enough to almost certainly have to experience the ashes, no, the war. The cloud is already there, all black on the horizon.

When we get home the rosy light of sunset lies on the snow. Our shadows are tall, and so are those of the ash trees along the road. Grandfather, key in hand, walks with steady steps toward the back door. He has cleared the snow away himself. The little boy throws himself on his back into the untrampled snow and makes an "angel." Soon the lawn is covered with little boy and girl "angels" in addition to the fan-like pattern made by pheasant wings and the hemstitch design made by mice.

And I know that I should say something about the war to all those who, like I, know that neither workers' rights of self-determination nor full employment will help us much when politicians one day let us know that they're "only human" and with many regrets inform us that the situation now is beyond their control, that peace is merely a period between two wars. Together we could accomplish much to sabotage the war effort.

But I place juniper branches into an earthenware jug, take some food out of the freezer, make a telephone call to an old lady in Stockholm, build a fire in the tiled stove. I live and function in my sleepy state; actually I've already fallen asleep, and the car is skidding into the ditch.

Only fifty meters from where we sit by candlelight in the dark of the night, while the children light sparklers in the apple trees and the moon rises across the stream, only fifty meters away, my typewriter is waiting, waiting, and I know that it won't have to carry out its troublesome assignment. Because for thousands of years a strange sleepiness has always overcome those who wanted to howl about how scared they were that human beings fully supported by the state and its bureaucracy would plan to start killing other human beings. There are words that remain unsaid. Deeds that are left unperformed.

For example, writing a fiery article against that war and world armament which is consuming us all like a secret sickness, its statistics showing us already lined up, submissive as sacrificial lambs—well, we still can escape, we still can die in a decent manner... But our children, poor things, how can they manage to get down into the deep, dark holes of the earth before the fire falls on their backs, softens their bones, and shrivels their small countenances into expressions of terror, such terror that we have not yet dared imagine it...

And we, who are so reluctant to allow them to light matches, afraid that they might get a little burn on their arms, we tolerate the fact that Europe's supply of hydrogen bombs is vast enough to spite all peace efforts, that there are politicians in this world who are short-sighted and callous enough to be able to use the concept of war as automatically as the butcher uses his axe... Just you wait, we'll be carved and tenderized all right, the way things look, but we don't even shiver. And besides, it doesn't concern us actually, since we perhaps aren't so impressed with what we are and the world we have produced...but the children, those whom we have lured into this labyrinth, can leave it only by means of death, what sort of death will it be? What sort of life? That's what it all amounts to.

And still, I know with my sleepy lizard eyes half closed, like an old dinosaur, that I will never approach that typewriter to write the only thing I must write, the only truth in my life (and in the lives of all those who, by means of radio, heard Hitler howl, and those who smelled the suffocating smoke of Auschwitz, just as those who are younger experienced the stench of burned stiff children, still moving, still terrified, running stiffly along the village roads of Vietnam—is there any difference between those roads and the roads between Runhallen and Vittinge?) The only truth in my life is writing against war.

The moon is rising over the rooftop now and makes the clouds shine like silver. From a distance the house sparkles and looks transparent. Some Telemann music is waiting on the piano to be played. The children are dancing around the kitchen floor, drunk with fatigue and chocolate pudding. The candles flicker feebly on the windowsill, one of them flares up like a nova and then goes out, reeking.

Like a house drawn in ashes. The blackened beams remain. Fires here and there. There were lots of fires long before man gave them a name. The fires will be there for a long time after we're gone. We build and live on top of the fire, we play with it, and some will be burned by it right in the middle of the most sensitive skin on their faces, and they won't be able to blink before their eyes are gone.

"Why was the bumble bee gone when we looked for it in its grave?"

"Resurrected on the third day," I chanted from the stove.

"Yes, but that was only the next day," the logical five-year-old objected from the kitchen bench.

"It's the maggots," the father said. "They eat up everything. Don't ever leave anything."

"And when you lay a dead person in the earth," the five-year-old says matter-of-factly, "the maggots come and. . ."

"Dinner is ready!" Grandmother called, and we all went into the dining room.

That was a long time ago. The moon is high up in the sky now, we can't tell the difference between planets and stars, they're all brilliant. We don't believe (we don't believe it to such an extent that we should actually say we don't at all know) that at this very moment people are suffering in torture chambers, worn out, their bodies destroyed, and mad with fear and humiliation, holding their crippled children in their arms, not much to bury, their lives crippled and destroyed, their existences smashed as by a sledge hammer.

I wake up in the middle of the night, the radiators are snapping, almost bursting with heat. A child mumbles in his sleep, a truck drives by and draws rapid designs of light on the white ceiling.

There was something I should do. But what was it? Something I should jot down, so as to write about it in greater detail tomorrow morning. I fumble for my writing pad and pencil, but can only find the little boy's empty cereal bowl. It was something about the children. And a danger. I get up and look at them. The moon is shining into their room. Outside, the trees are sparkling. The girl has put her chubby leg on top of the blanket to cool off. The little boy is lying on his back, his arms stretched up over the pillow, as though to make another angel in the snow.

The sleeping people's breathing seems to make the whole house whisper. Above it the starry sky sparkles. Nothing can very well happen here. If there was anything I was supposed to write, it'll have to wait until morning. And I let myself fall into sleep like a stone. There will be no rings on the surface.